# SECRETS AT PARATA BAY

SOPHIE HAYDON

BAY BOOKS

**Secrets at Parata Bay**
by Sophie Haydon

*A grieving mother intent on revenge. A millionaire who values honesty above all else. A love threatened by the legacy of family...*

—**The Mackenzies**—
A Place Called Home
Secrets at Parata Bay
Escape to Shelter Springs
What you See in the Stars
Second Chance at Whisper Creek
Summer at the Lakehouse Café

—**Lantern Bay**—
Yours to Give
Yours to Treasure
Yours to Cherish
Yours to Keep
Yours Forever
Yours to Love

For more at https://sophiehaydon.com

ISBN 978-199-102106-9 (Amazon Print)
ISBN 978-199-102125-0 (Draft2Digital Print)

# CONTENTS

## CHAPTER ONE

"Come in!" The low growl penetrated the thick oak door effortlessly.

It was an order. It was without finesse. It was exactly what Cassandra had expected.

Even so, her hand trembled slightly as she smoothed her straightened hair, pushing a stubborn curl firmly behind her ear. She had to have everything under control if she was going to succeed.

She opened the heavy door, allowing it to swing wide before she made her entrance. It had to be a good one; she would have only one chance.

With a quick glance she scanned the dark office registering the minimal decor, clear desk, single light pooled over a closed laptop, before her eyes rested on the man whose image haunted her every waking moment—Dallas Mackenzie.

He stood in shadow with his back to her, hands thrust in pockets, staring out over the lights of Wellington.

"What do you want?"

He hadn't even bothered to turn to face her. Fear flickered in her gut. "I've come to be interviewed for the PA position."

"I'm not interviewing today. Come back tomorrow with the others."

She swallowed. "I can't. It has to be today. The agency rang and arranged the appointment with your receptionist for 5.30." Her first lie. It had been easier than she'd thought.

"You're late then."

He still hadn't turned around.

"I'm not late. I've been waiting over an hour."

Cassandra walked slowly towards him and stopped in the middle of the room, suddenly confronted with her own image clearly visible in the window against the darkening sky. It was an image she didn't recognize—sleekly groomed and in control.

He grunted but still didn't move, simply continued to stare across the darkening harbor towards the Rimutaka ranges, glowing orange in the setting sun.

She had to admit the view was incredible. No wonder the man felt invincible. He had the city at his feet. Just a pity he chose to abuse his power. But that was where she came in, wasn't it?

"Go home."

"You're too busy to see me? Fine." She turned and walked away, her stilettos ringing out on the marble floor. "But you need to know you're passing up the best opportunity you'll get of employing a good PA. I know, I've looked through the CVs of the other candidates and they won't last."

She stopped by the door. The thud of her heart seemed to shake her body with its intensity. All the work of these past months in preparation for this moment. Was it all for nothing? She had to see. She turned her head just enough to check his reaction.

He'd shifted slightly, briefly revealing his profile against the city lights, before turning to her. An advertising hoarding cast alternating beams of red and green light across his cheek bone and down to the hard set of his mouth. The effect was demonic and unnerving. Although his eyes remained in darkness, Cassandra's skin prickled under their intense scrutiny.

He sighed: a deep soul-wrenching sigh. "I'm not too busy."

For a fleeting moment Cassandra felt the shock of the unexpected. She thought she recognized the emptiness behind the sound. One look at his arrogant face and the thought vanished as quickly as it came.

"I asked my receptionist to tell you to leave. She obviously decided not to."

She turned to face him. "So you'll interview me now?"

"Doesn't look as if I have much choice does it, Miss..."

She stepped towards him and offered her hand.

"Lee. Cassandra Lee." She smiled tentatively, trying to contain her nerves.

He didn't smile back but took her hand in his. Rather than dispelling her nerves the warmth and strength of his hand briefly engulfing hers, shook her. She felt his power, and from the way his gray eyes narrowed slowly, she also felt his interest.

"The agency rang, you say?"

She nodded.

"Really?"

A warning shiver trickled down her back at the lowered

tone. Her lie hadn't gone undetected. But she had no choice but to continue.

"You wanted someone 'highly organized, experienced and prepared for anything—24/7.'"

"And I take it you're all that?"

"And more. I also have superb references, a Masters degree and I'm a creative thinker."

*Particularly when it came to her CV.* She dropped a copy of the document—more fiction than fact—on to his desk.

"In case you didn't receive a copy from the agency."

He didn't move.

"What I want to know about an employee, a CV can't tell me."

"And that is?"

"I work on gut instinct."

He walked slowly across the room and flicked on a light before turning towards her once more.

She could see him more clearly now: longish dark hair threaded with gray, a face strong and powerful rather than handsome. He had the face and body of a street fighter, deceptively relaxed but ready for anything. He also had the demeanor of a fighter: rude, arrogant and instinctive. And all this, dressed in an immaculate suit that shouted establishment. He was a contradiction.

But above all that she could see the keen intelligence in his eyes that now were narrowed and focused on her as though he could read her soul. A pity she couldn't read his. Gut instinct wasn't something for which she'd been able to prepare. "And what's your gut instinct telling you now?"

He stepped towards her. "That you're a determined woman who wants this job badly for some reason."

She stepped back. She was cornered and had no other

option than to come out fighting. "How can you possibly tell that from our brief conversation?"

He ignored her question and leaned back against the desk, folding his arms. "Who are you and why do you want this job so badly you'd lie to get it?"

She controlled the pulse of fear at his words. Fear could destroy everything she'd worked towards. She needed to be strong. She knew instinctively that he was a man who would despise weakness. She held his gaze. "You're right, I didn't go through the agency. I wanted to be first in line, to show you why I'm the best applicant. I want this job."

"Sit down Miss Lee and we'll talk. I'll get you a drink."

As she sat down on the hard leather chair, she breathed a deep sigh of relief. She'd got through to him. He was giving her a chance.

Cassandra noted his hospitality didn't extend to asking her what she'd like to drink as he poured a glass of wine and a large glass of soda water.

After passing her the glass of wine he sat back, took a long drink of soda water and picked up his cell phone.

She waited for him to speak.

And waited.

She could only marvel at his ability to ignore the niceties of polite conversation as he loosened his tie, rolled up his shirt sleeves and replied to a couple of messages with short cursory answers.

Since passing her a drink, he'd appeared to put her out of his mind: as important as a piece of paper in his in-tray that could wait until he was ready to deal with it.

Unfortunately it was long enough for Cassandra's focus to waver. The sight of Dallas Mackenzie loosening his clothing did something to her that she was glad he was too self-absorbed to witness. None of her preparations had included how to cope with a quickened heartbeat at the sight of his bare chest as he dragged down the knot of his tie, inadvertently popping a button open.

She took a hasty gulp of wine to calm her racing pulse and smoothed the velvety condensation on the glass with her finger as she tried to fathom the source of the attraction.

She looked up from beneath lowered lashes as he rolled up his sleeves. It could have been the way his shirt pulled over his shoulders, revealing the hard contours of his body. It could have been his chest. He obviously worked out, but not too much. The muscles lay lean under his skin.

Her eyes dropped. No, for some reason that Cassandra could not fathom, it was his forearms. She stared once more at the exposed arm—tanned and strong, its muscles bunched and tactile. She could imagine how it would feel cupped by her palm. But it wasn't just a sensuous response. She knew that this was the real man—the ruthless man who would stop at nothing to get what he wanted—behind the smooth, sophisticated suit. A shiver ran down her spine. She didn't want to see the real man. She had a job to do.

And it wasn't the one he thought she was here for.

After several long minutes he flung down the cell phone and turned to her abruptly as he reached for his glass.

"Your health. Miss Lee."

"Cassandra, please."

"Cassandra." He nodded and took a sip of his soda water, placing it carefully on the table before sitting back in the leather chair. His face was caught in a half-shadow cast by the oversized lampshade that hung between them. But she could see that he was interested in her. It didn't matter for what reason. Whether it was her body or her mind, and she didn't kid herself it was the latter, it didn't matter. What was important was that she got the job and to do that she had to be bold, no holds barred.

"So, what brings an American girl to New Zealand?"

She leaned forward, meeting his direct gaze, watching for his response.

"Unfinished business." She felt, instinctively, that the truth or some version of it, would pique his interest more effectively than some facile, predictable response. But when his eyes narrowed she suddenly realized he was too suspicious to leave her answer open to interpretation. "My mother has relatives here and I also had someone I needed to see. The unfinished business... it was, personal." She hoped that her lowered tone and shy glance would satisfy his curiosity.

He tilted his head to one side, his eyes still narrowed, unconvinced. "Really?"

"I guess you could say that love drove me here."

"Love?" His eyes betrayed no flicker of emotion and his lips, no hint of a smile. "For love you'd move countries?"

"People will do a lot for love."

He half-laughed. "Then they're crazy. Love is an over-rated state."

"Maybe. But it's often hard to control."

"Is yours?"

"My feelings are," she hesitated only momentarily, "totally under control."

"So why is a beautiful woman, in love with her man, sitting here with me after six o'clock? I asked for a PA without a life. I need someone with me 24/7—it's a live-in job. There can be no distractions."

"There are none." Again, the truth.

"Not such a happy ending after all then?"

"Happy ever after is for fairy stories, not real life and in real life I need a job. I need, I want, this job. I've been wanting to work with you for some time."

He rested his elbows on the table between them and steepled his fingers, strong capable looking fingers, before his face. For the first time Cassandra noticed that the tip of his right index finger was missing. She glanced up quickly but not before he'd noticed the direction of her gaze. His eyes, still in the shadow of the low light, were cold, watchful.

"Have you now? And why is that?"

*Revenge.* The single word slammed through her mind. But there was a limit to the amount of truth she could tell him.

"I'm looking for a challenge." She crossed her legs, the stockings skimming against each other as she smoothed her skirt over her thighs. "And I think you're it."

His eyes fell briefly to her legs before returning to her face. His expression was unreadable, his eyes, cold.

"I know the business inside out and I have the qualifications. I want, now, to work on the strategic side. I can give you what you need." She paused for effect but saw no trace of emotion on his face. "And you can give me something too. Experience at the top level."

She shifted slightly and saw a glimmer of something akin to recognition in his eyes.

He leaned back in his chair, watching her openly, probing, assessing and finally judging. She could see that he'd come to some kind of decision about her. But she'd have to wait to find out what it was.

"A mutually beneficial relationship, you think?"

"I know."

"I don't. Not yet. You *appear* to have everything I want."

She blinked lightly. Dallas Mackenzie was one disturbing man, but he would never have the satisfaction of knowing he was unsettling her. She was the one to gain satisfaction from this relationship, not him.

"But?"

"There's something..." his eyes narrowed and he sat back into the chair, his disturbing gaze not leaving hers for a moment, "missing."

Cassandra's eyes widened. She couldn't help herself. She hadn't anticipated this. What had she forgotten? She swallowed, hoping he wouldn't notice the fear that was threatening to break through her carefully constructed façade.

"Look, I apologize for the unusual tactic, beating the agency to the job."

"I'm not concerned about that."

"What is it then. What's missing?" She tried to sound cool, keep her voice low and controlled.

The way his eyes searched her face told her that he didn't buy her story.

"I don't know yet. But I will."

She had to have the job.

"Perhaps you should give me the chance to show you how I work?"

He nodded. "Good idea. How about a trial—say for a week—and then we'll see how we both feel?"

Her heart sank. Where had she slipped up?

She forced herself to smile. Perhaps she could do it in a week anyway.

"That sounds great. When shall I start?"

"How does right now sound?"

Without waiting for her answer he opened the laptop and spun it round to face her.

"Your first assignment. I, or rather *we*, have a meeting in a few days and I want to be prepared. Use this," he tapped the laptop "and this," he reached over and touched her head "and prepare a report in half an hour. Any questions?"

Fighting the distraction of his touch, forcing herself to concentrate, she leaned forward and scanned the contents of the proposal. At last, something she could get her teeth into.

"No. I'll let you have a report in half an hour."

He raised his eyebrows. "Good. There will be someone outside if you need anything. I'll be back in quarter of an hour. Have it ready for me then. Because if you haven't, the deal's off."

She wanted to hit him. She nodded instead.

He finished his drink and strode out of the room, jacket slung casually over one shoulder.

No problem, you bastard, thought Cassandra, as she began scanning the proposal before quickly flicking back to the internet to run some financial searches. Alone in his office at last. How she'd imagined this. But now wasn't the time for self-congratulation or hacking into his security network and company databases, now was a time to earn some trust. Lucky she knew his business inside out, probably better than he did.

Dallas took a deep breath of the sweet evening air and looked around Mackenzie Square—his square.

He walked slowly over to the garden at the centre of the square. He glanced briefly at the cluster of mothers who watched their children play in the small playground he'd been persuaded to include. His gaze didn't linger. It was an alien world to him and always would be. They'd be gone soon, home to their families. Not for him. *Never* for him.

He sat heavily on the empty bench under the gnarled branches of the ancient pohutukawa tree where once Maori canoes had beached. That was before the seabed had been reclaimed and mirrored giants rose, dwarfing the tree, changing the landscape forever.

Looking up through the tree's twisted limbs Dallas contemplated his own mirrored giant. More beautiful than most, maybe, but complete and therefore of no further interest to him. Unlike Miss Lee. She interested him greatly.

Sitting back, elbows resting on the seat behind him, he felt interest stir in his veins, replacing the emptiness that had engulfed him since the completion of the project. He'd known it would arrive eventually. Just hadn't pictured it arriving in the form of a tall, slim brunette.

He focused on his office window, fifteen floors above, and smiled to himself.

———

One hour later Dallas returned.

"Ready?"

"Yes." She swallowed her annoyance and retrieved the report from the printer and handed it to him.

He scanned the papers. "Pretty thorough for such a short time."

"At first glance it looks good. There's no hint of any foreign competitor joining the market. The company's traditional, solid and would be worth investing in." She frowned. "But I'd need to know what"—she glanced at the covering notes—"John Stewart's plans for the company are if you want a more informative report."

"We'll leave it there for now. Good start. Do some more work on it tomorrow. In the meantime, if you're free, I'd like you to join me at a cocktail party to welcome the Australian ambassador. I want you to meet a few people, get to know some of my business colleagues who'll be there."

"Tonight? Yes, that's fine. But I don't have anything to wear. I've left my suitcase at the InterContinental Hotel."

She could feel Dallas's eyes trail slowly over her body.

"You're fine. You can freshen up upstairs in my apartment if you wish and then we'll leave. I'll have Todd pick up your case later."

"What time do we have to be there?"

"When we get there."

Why was she not surprised by his answer?

"So I'm your new PA?"

He nodded. "A week's trial and then we'll see."

He stood up and they shook hands.

"That's it? No contract, no confidentiality clauses?"

He punched the button of a private lift.

"You can sort that out for me tomorrow. In the meantime I suggest you get ready. You don't want to be late. Just one more thing. You lied to get the job. Okay, you got my attention. But don't ever lie to me again, or else you'll be out."

She nodded stiffly. "Of course." Another lie.

The elevator doors swept open and stood waiting for her.

She hesitated, for just one brief moment, knowing she was walking into danger. She'd have to be alert. Because she knew exactly where that danger lay: in this man, charismatic, arrogant, and sexy as hell.

*The man responsible for the death of her father and her son.*

Then she smiled up at him and entered the lift, dimly aware of the echo of her heels stabbing the marble floor with their metallic tips. The elevator doors closed with a whisper, ending the months of waiting, the months of pain.

## CHAPTER TWO

Dallas heard the guest bedroom door open and close quietly behind him. He dropped Cassandra's report on to the desk, flicked out the light and turned to look out the window.

"Come here."

He could smell her light, fresh perfume before she arrived beside him.

"Look down there. What do you see?"

"The Mackenzie Building. Winner of the Architectural Futures Award, built in record time, earner of the highest rents in the capital. Your building."

He smiled wryly. "That just about covers it."

"You must feel proud of a job well done."

He should, but he didn't. He couldn't feel anything. That was the problem. Money had been his exclusive focus for so many years that little else registered. And now the project was finished—the completion of years of work, years of dreaming—and he felt, nothing. But then he'd gone out of his way to stay aloof from feelings for more years than he cared to remember.

"Indeed."

"And your next project?"

"Ah, that's where you come in."

He turned to his new PA, the irresistible Cassandra, and took in the immaculate make-up, the seductive camisole that barely covered her cleavage. Possibly just the diversion he needed to fill the void of emptiness and despair that threatened to engulf him.

The diversionary tactics seemed to be working already. He'd just spent a pleasurable ten minutes listening to the hum of the shower and giving his imagination full rein. The image of a naked, dripping Cassandra, soaping her body ran a close second to the fully clothed woman beside him.

"Where exactly do I come in?"

He could tell by the light flush that gathered on her pale cheeks that she didn't know which way to take this. But then, nor did he.

"Your first task will be to assess the proposals that have been piling up. I haven't had the time, or the inclination, and unfortunately I've had a little trouble with PAs."

"I guess it might be best if I know what the problem is with your PAs. I might stand a chance of avoiding it."

"Sure. It's simple. Don't think I'm ever going to marry you, Cassandra, because you haven't a hope in hell."

For a second, he regretted his words, could tell that she was angry and hurt at his presumption. But, whatever. It was the truth and if she couldn't take the truth, then she could leave.

"Well, lucky for you that I have no wish to marry you then, isn't it? Shall we go?"

"Sure." He could see the effect of his words on her. No doubt she thought him a cold and arrogant bastard which was all to the good because he was. Any softening he'd sensed in her before had now vanished.

He enjoyed the sight of Cassandra walking towards the door, her tightly skirted behind arousing his libido in ways he'd almost forgotten. There was no doubt about it. He needed something to divert him from the fact he was alone and always would be. He could never trust himself to marry, to become a man like his father. Cassandra could be just the thing.

She stopped at the elevator and turned to look up at him.

He had been admiring her rear view and made no sudden attempt to change the direction of his gaze. Lazily he looked up into her eyes, reached one arm towards and past her, and pressed the elevator button. The door clicked open.

"After you."


Spring in Wellington was usually a brisk affair but tonight the wind had dropped and the air was mild. Cassandra could even smell the spring flowers that were planted in drifts around the spreading pohutukawa tree. An unusual choice for Mackenzie Square. But Dallas Mackenzie was an unusual man.

Mackenzie Square. The man had to put his stamp on everything.

A powerful man. The sort of man no-one in their right mind would cross. So what was she doing? She was playing with fire and she could feel the heat smoldering within, simply in response to his fluid movements beside her, simply at the sense of the containment of his power, his sexuality.

She shot him a quick look and wished she hadn't. He'd stepped in front of her to press the intercom to speak to the porter at the embassy gates and she couldn't help noticing the way his dark hair curled lightly into the nape of his neck, resting on the crisp white shirt collar. It was the kind of hair that you wanted to run your fingers through: coiling a curl round a finger and dragging down its silky length before releasing it once more.

She licked her lips and swallowed, hoping she'd find her voice and her self-control before he looked around.

The small gate buzzed and swung open. He stepped to one side to allow her to pass.

"Thanks." Her voice was huskier than normal. She chanced a brief look that met narrowed eyes. He didn't miss a trick.

----

What was it with women and talking? Some of them never stopped.

Dallas glanced down at the constantly moving mouth of the ambassador's wife and wondered briefly why on earth she should think he would be interested in her past work experiences. Something to do with opera or England. Who knew? Who could follow? Who would want to?

But the continuous drone didn't seem to require any response on his part so he let her words flow over him, unimpeded, just as the sight of Cassandra shimmering under the soft lights, flowed through his veins.

For the first time in weeks, he felt interested in something. Unfortunately, it wasn't business. His mind was on pleasure: pleasure with Cassandra. And who wouldn't be attracted to her? But it wasn't just looks. There was something odd, something misplaced and mysterious that intrigued him.

But, as much as he wanted a diversion, his first need was a good PA and this woman had brains. He also needed to see if she had intuition. He'd find that out tonight.

Business or pleasure, which would it be? He knew there was no real choice. His business must always flourish. He owed it to his mother and brothers. He'd sworn to make up for his father's excesses, rebuild his family fortunes, and he'd never renege on that promise.

A lull in the overall buzz in conversation made him vaguely aware that his hostess had moved on from opera to children. Of even less interest to him, if that were possible.

Good. Cassandra was talking to an old friend of his. It would be interesting to watch her deal with him.


"So Cassandra, you're Dallas's new PA. What's your background?"

"Project management mainly. Plus some research in information systems." No lies exactly but Cassandra knew more would be read into it than actually existed.

"Lucky old Dallas." She didn't believe his comment was a reflection on her work experience from the way his eyes kept descending to her breasts.

"And you are...?"

He smiled and she saw he'd been an attractive man once. "John Stewart, old friend of Dallas's."

"Ah." She nodded, recognizing the name of the man behind the investment proposal she'd investigated earlier.

"Yep, we've got ourselves into a few scrapes in the past. Had ourselves a lot of fun." He knocked back his whiskey and scanned the room. "Times change though." His edgy look wasn't lost on her. There was a feeling of desperation about him and, from the tense expression on his face as he looked over at Dallas once more, she could see that he was looking to him for his financial salvation.

She joined John's gaze to find Dallas's eyes were trained on her, despite the fact the ambassador's wife was talking to him, oblivious to Dallas's evident lack of interest.

It was as if a match had been struck within her, instantly sending flames of fire through her body, licking the nerve endings on her skin and keeping the incendiary embers glowing, white-hot, deep inside. She moved her glass, clinking with ice cubes, under her face, relishing the cool air that wafted up to her heated cheeks.

She couldn't turn away. Shocked by the instinctive, primitive response of her body to his gaze, she desperately wanted to break the connection, to shift gears, to allow her mind to regain control. But she couldn't. His eyes, warming by the second, held her in thrall. Somewhere in the deep recesses of her mind, she knew she should hate him, knew she was here for a purpose and this wasn't it. But at that moment her body wanted him—pure and simple—and refused to be guided. His mouth curved slowly into a smile, and his eyes lit with a gleam as he registered her response.

It wasn't until Cassandra felt a damp hand slide around her waist, that she was jerked back into the moment. She turned to see John's face too close, and forced herself to smile, forced herself back into the *now*. "It was nice meeting you, John." She twisted round, plucked a glass from a passing tray, and slipped away.

Dallas watched as Cassandra casually and effectively rejected his old friend's unwanted attentions. He smiled. It was coolly, if not a bit abruptly, done.

He placed his empty glass on the table decisively. If she was good, then it was business and he had to stay clear. If not, then anything went, so long as she knew it was only temporary. And so long as he also remembered that too. He had a nasty feeling if he started up some sort of liaison with Cassandra, it wouldn't be so easy to stop.

But he wouldn't rush his decision. He'd enjoy toying with the idea, for tonight at least. He'd take her to dinner, find out a bit more about her.

"And so here I am. About to re-launch my career."

He looked up surprised and then remembered that his hostess had been talking to him and had now paused. It seemed a suitable response was required.

"Your career? And what is that?"

It was his hostess's turn to look puzzled.

"Opera singing. I've just been telling you about it."

"Oh." The pause lengthened. "Good."

He smiled, hoping this would provide whatever acknowledgement his hostess required and moved on to join Cassandra, unperturbed by the exasperated snort from behind him.


"Cassandra!" Dallas wanted to reach out and press his fingers into the curve of her lower back, to let his thumb gently push up under her jacket and feel the silky camisole beneath. He kept his hands firmly in his pockets. "Dinner?"

"Sounds good. Where?"

The loud hum of chatter made it necessary for him to lean down to catch her response and breathe in her perfume. The sultry, yet fresh smell conjured up visions of intimate tumbling in poppy-strewn corn fields under a hot sun. He lost his train of thought.

"Where, what?"

"Are we going?" She looked up at him sharply, as if she could read his mind. He was going to have to watch himself.

He drew back a little. "A restaurant nearby. I'm hungry and I've had enough small talk."

"Fine." She curved her lips to form a slightly crooked smile. "I'll try not to make my talk too small then."

He grinned and indicated the way out. "So long as you don't talk about your family history or babies, you'll be okay."

He wondered why the smile suddenly vanished from those beautiful lips and she turned away, but mentally shrugged. Who knew what went on in a woman's mind?

As they threaded their way to the door, John suddenly appeared before them, swaying, his eyes unfocused and reddened.

"So, Dallas, tell me what you think of my proposal."

"Cassandra has looked into it for me."

John turned suddenly interested eyes to Cassandra.

"Good business deal. You won't find better."

"It's not just about the bottom line though, John, is it?"

Dallas was sure that the coolness he detected in her voice had as much to do with John's unfocused gaze on her breasts as it did with the business deal.

"The deal needs to stack up on every level," Cassandra continued. "Dallas won't want to be involved in anything that could compromise his reputation.'

"What do you mean?"

She smiled lightly. He could see it was a smile designed

to hide her true thoughts. "There's more research to be done."

She was good. Dallas could tell her previous research had been tempered by her face to face meeting with John. She obviously wasn't impressed.

He suddenly felt irritated and looked away from her. She was too good to lose. He'd been looking for a good PA for years. He couldn't do anything to jeopardize this. But that was tomorrow. He'd enjoy tonight first.

"Dallas?" John's voice had been edgy before but now held an aggressive undertone that triggered memories Dallas preferred to forget. "Come on! You're not going to leave our business negotiations to this, *girl*, who knows nothing. You're not going to let her advise you on your business? Why don't we let her go and powder her nose and we can get down to business?"

"Cassandra's part of the business now. Leave it until tomorrow. We'll discuss it when you're sober."

"And you'd know all about sobriety, wouldn't you, Dallas?"

Anger burned in Dallas's gut, sending blood pounding through his body.

"I'd stop right there, if I were you." Dallas clenched and unclenched his fists.

"Well you're not me, are you? Not any more. Not like the old days, eh?" John tried to grab Dallas's hand, to show his missing finger. "See that Cassandra? How do you think he got that? Not by sipping bloody soda water, that's for sure. Nor by hanging out in board rooms on his best behavior."

"We'll talk tomorrow." Dallas turned away and went outside with Cassandra, willing the blood-red pulsing in his veins to cease. It was only when the cool air hit him in the empty street that he stopped walking and passed the phone to Cassandra.

"Call Todd, tell him we've had a change of plan. We won't be needing him for a few hours." He dimly registered the quiet control in his voice that didn't reflect the blind anger he felt inside—it never had.

"What's wrong with now?" John called from behind them, the aggression in his voice impossible to ignore.

"It's not the time, nor the place. Leave it." He began to walk away. *He could do this.*

"Cassandra's talking nonsense, mate. Don't listen to her. Don't mix business with pleasure. If you want, f—"

In one swift movement Dallas was upon him, his fist tight around John's collar, pinning him to the wall. But not quickly enough to prevent John from describing in obscene terms what Dallas could do to Cassandra. Dallas could barely hear Cassandra's voice above the pounding of his own blood. The primitive urge to fight was all consuming.

It was the fear in John's eyes that finally penetrated his fury, prompting him to release John from his grip.

"Don't ever talk to me, or Cassandra, like that again John because, if you do, that will be the end. No more business."

"Sure, sure." John pulled his jacket back into shape.

"Look, I'm sorry." Dallas pushed fingers through his hair, both angry and sorry that he'd been goaded into losing control. "We go back a long way John, and I owe you. But don't push me again."

"That's all I want Dallas. I want to do business with you, not some girl."

"You're drunk, John. I'll see you in a few days and we can discuss business then."

He walked away and Cassandra fell into step beside him.

It took the length of the empty street before Dallas felt calm enough to speak. He turned to Cassandra for the first time.

"I apologize for John." He hesitated only a moment. "And I apologize for me." What on earth was he doing? What kind of effect was this woman having on him? He never apologized for anything.

"You don't have to apologize for someone else's behavior." They walked on a few more steps.

He waited to see if she would comment on his own apology. She didn't.

---

The restaurant had once been a private villa. Prestigiously perched on the hills overlooking the glittering harbor, the grand old house now catered for patrons who desired privacy and were used to the best. And Dallas often enjoyed the discretion it offered. Never more so than now, as he sat back and watched Cassandra order her dinner from the waiter.

She was an enigma and it only intrigued him more.

The usual response to an apology—especially by a new employee—would have been either a polite rejection of its necessity, or a polite acceptance. Which meant Cassandra was neither acquiescent nor polite. Despite a slightly ruffled ego, he liked that.

He also liked the way her straight, dark hair shone in the candlelight, revealing subtle highlights that couldn't be reproduced in a hair salon. The depth of color provided a stunning foil to her pale skin and deep blue eyes. Irish coloring, he guessed. Wherever her family originated from, she was very beautiful.

He took a sip of soda water and placed it carefully back onto the table between them, as he tried to control his visceral reaction to her. He looked up and caught her gaze. He realized his attempt at control had failed; he was incredibly attracted to her. Years ago, he would simply have taken her back to his apartment and they would have made love all night. But he had the feeling one night wouldn't be enough.

His errant thoughts of how much fun pleasuring this woman would be, were interrupted by the waiter bringing the drinks and responding to Cassandra's enquiry about the restaurant's history.

Dallas only half listened as his eyes wandered back to Cassandra. Her chin was tilted up as she looked at the waiter, revealing her long neck which, God help him, he had an irrational desire to lick. Her hair fell, straight as a die, down her ramrod straight back. There was a slight stiffness to her elegance as if she were conscious of every movement, not entirely at ease. When the waiter left and she turned back to catch his gaze, he could see the unease in her eyes too. She was holding something back, but he'd find out what it was. Later.

"So, John Stewart. Do you want me to continue to research his proposal?" Her voice was business like and cool, telling quite a different story to the look in her eyes.

Of all the things he wanted to talk about, work wasn't one of them.

"Sure. John and I go back a long way. He's hit hard times and wants some financial backing. Check it out for me."

She nodded. "I also heard talk of a couple of things tonight that were of interest."

"What things?"

"He was mentioned in connection with a company notorious for asset stripping. Are you interested in that?"

"Not as a rule. But never say never. Do some more research on it and get back to me tomorrow."

"Sure. I just didn't get a good feel from him about the project."

It was as he thought. She was too good to lose.

"So, tell me, Cassandra, what it is that you get a good feel from? What is it that pleases the aloof Miss Lee?"

She raised an eyebrow in brief query at his deliberate choice of words. "Doing my job well."

"That's it?"

"That's all I assume you'd be interested in."

"You assume incorrectly. Tell me about yourself."

"Where to begin?"

"With your dancing?"

"How did you know I danced?"

"I can tell by how you hold yourself. Ballet?"

"It was. An injury put pay to that."

"Were you disappointed?"

"Of course. Ballet was my life."

"An early disappointment then. What next?"

"Study. Finance and management."

He waved a hand to dismiss these subjects. He wanted to know about her. "Where were you born and raised?"

"Massachusetts. Nothing much else to say. It was a happy, comfortable upbringing; I then went on to have a happy, comfortable marriage to a good man who died, and, a few months ago, I came to New Zealand. End of story."

"Or, perhaps, just the beginning. I take it you're now looking for something other than 'happy and comfortable?'"

"Most people would have responded with 'I'm sorry to hear of your husband's death.'"

He shrugged. "I'm not most people. I'm sorry if your happiness was curtailed but, you know, somehow I wonder if it was." Her lips pursed briefly and her glance flicked away, showing an irritation that up till now she'd managed to hide. "I've annoyed you."

She took a studied sip of her wine. "No. You can imagine what you like. You're not to know the truth."

He narrowed his eyes. He didn't know anything about her past, about her happiness or otherwise. He was just guessing of course. But her phrasing was odd. Her last words sounded more like a directive than an observation.

"Shame. Because truth is very important to me. And it should be to you, too, while you're in my employ."

Her blue eyes were dark as slate as he met her gaze. "Of course. So I have the job?"

Again, the prevarication, the lack of a direct answer. "For a trial period, as I said. I've not made up my mind about you yet. It will also give you a chance to better understand how I work."

"I know how you work."

"Really?" He shook his head, at a loss to understand how. "Hearsay? Tabloid headlines? That sort of thing."

She took her time eating a mouthful of food before she answered. He made the most of that time watching her perfect lips move exquisitely as she chewed the tender chicken, and her throat constrict as she swallowed. He glanced up to see that she'd noticed where his attention lay.

"That sort of thing," she replied without haste. "And more. So much is available on the internet, so that even from the other side of the world one can watch the progress of business and its players, one can analyze their moves as one would a chess player and one can form judgments."

"I'm flattered that you paid such minute attention to me. Tell me, why?"

"Your property developments are renowned for their innovation and quality. And"—she paused briefly—"from the moment I learned of your latest developments, I've wanted to work with you."

Something didn't sit right. "If you're trying to flatter me, it's not working. Tell me about your other reasons for coming to New Zealand."

She didn't look up at him immediately and he thought he saw her hand shake slightly before she placed her fork carefully on the plate and dropped her hands to her lap. Then she looked up at him with the full force of her calm, blue gaze.

"My mother had New Zealand connections, I've been wanting to come here since I heard her stories as a child. And, as I mentioned earlier, I had someone in particular I came to see."

"Hmm. Killing two birds with one stone." He could have sworn she blanched as a sheen of cool sweat settled on her forehead. But her eyes barely registered the change her skin revealed.

"I think that about sums up my reason for being here."

There was a long pause while Dallas wondered whether he should push for an explanation. But he was enjoying the intrigue too much to want it to end. There was a lot to be said for prolonging the journey, the process, the foreplay. He wasn't in any hurry to reach that point where the fascination evaporated into a mirage of dust leaving only emptiness. He finished his soda water. No hurry at all. He glanced at his watch.

"Time we were off."

"Where to?"

"Home with me. 24/7 remember."

"I assumed I'd be staying close to your office, on call."

"You assumed wrongly. I've tried that and it didn't work. From now on my PA stays with me, at my house."

"I hope you haven't got the wrong idea about me."

"I doubt it very much."

"I won't be sleeping with you."

He laughed. "So candid and direct. I can't tell you that it hasn't crossed my mind. But I don't always act on every passing thought." He stood up and pulled the chair from her as she rose, before stepping back. "But this is business. If you still want the job?"

"I do."

"I want you to be with me, 24/7, so we can get on with the business of making money. Agreed?"

"Agreed."

"Ready to be on-call twenty-four hours a day for the next seven days?"

She nodded. "Sure." Her clipped reply betrayed a reluctance to which she obviously refused to succumb.

"I'd assumed you'd agree. Todd has already collected your case from the hotel. He's waiting for us." He looked up into the night sky. "It'll be a fine ride to the Bay."

# CHAPTER THREE

The Bay. His home. This was it. The beginning.

It was a short walk through the empty streets back to the Mackenzie Building and a silent one. The odd glance Cassandra cast at Dallas showed him to be lost in thought and apparently fixated on the pavement ahead. He walked quickly, withdrawn into his own world and oblivious to the fact she was having trouble keeping up with him. The tight skirt and the ridiculously high heels were keeping her a good few paces behind him and she was trailing fast.

Not a good look she decided as she attempted to run a couple of steps to make up the ground. But just as she reached him, her foot twisted slightly, sending her flying in front of him.

As the pavement loomed up in slow motion in front of her eyes, she cried out in surprise and his arm smoothly plucked her from the fall, drawing her to his body.

She could feel his heart pound with the sudden shot of adrenalin as her cheek rubbed against his satiny-smooth lapel.

"You okay?" He pulled her up to standing and held her close as he searched her face in concern.

She nodded, embarrassed at the sudden proximity and at the reason for it.

"Sorry, not used to the heels."

She regretted the words as soon as they left her lips. She'd given something away and his eyes lit up with interest.

"Really? Your previous position more of a flat shoes kind of job?"

"Something like that. Luckily the height of my heels didn't affect my job performance."

"Then why bother with them for me? Trying to impress? Or something else?"

He didn't have to spell it out. He imagined she was trying to seduce him.

"Of course I was trying to impress. It was a job interview." She tried to pull away, grateful for the timely reminder of his arrogance. It distracted her from the touch of his hand—hot through her thin jacket—and the tilt of his usually stern lips, now parted slightly, torn between amusement and arousal. He also smelt divine—a blend of aftershave, outdoors and pure maleness. But he wouldn't let her move. And somehow, she didn't want to.

Long seconds passed before he let his hands stroke down her arms and then drop free.

"You're a woman of contradictions, Cassandra Lee. I think I've got you figured out and then you go and surprise me."

"How so?"

"A dancer who is both graceful"—he grinned, a disarming and all too rare grin—"and clumsy."

She stiffened. "I haven't danced in years."

"Shame. I bet you were good at it."

She nodded. "Perhaps, at one time. But now there's only one thing you need to know about me." She wouldn't back down from his gaze. "And that's that I'm good at my job."

"I could see that tonight. You worked the room well, you mixed easily with everyone there, John included. He's not the easiest of people." His mouth tightened once more.

"Then why do business with him?"

"As I said, we go back a long way. He used to bail me out of trouble when I was younger. I owe him. Even though we've been going separate ways for some years now, I never forget where my loyalties lie." He offered his arm to her. She paused briefly before taking it.

"I don't want you lunging after me again. People may get the wrong idea."

She sent him an irritated look, but fell into step beside him.

"No doubt you think I did it on purpose."

"No. Somehow I don't think a dancer of your grace could ever purposely be so inelegant."

"Why, thank you for the back-handed compliment."

"My pleasure." He stopped in front of the building and paused to retrieve his security card. "Sounds like Todd is ready for us."

Suddenly she was aware of the sound of rotor-blades slicing the night air high above her. She looked up to see a helicopter warming its engine on the roof. Bright landing lights revealed the shiny red body of the craft, toy-like against a backdrop of dark sky that was slowly lightening with the silver smudge of a rising moon.

A helicopter. Of course. She knew he owned one but had conveniently forgotten she'd be expected to fly in one.

She swallowed hard. She hated helicopters.

But she had no choice. It was the next stage of the journey: a journey, she was increasingly feeling, into unchartered territory.

———

"You want to take the controls yourself, sir?"

"No, not tonight, Todd. It's all yours. I've got, er"—he couldn't resist a glimpse of her long, slender legs—"business to attend to."

"So I can see sir."

He sat back, relaxed, and acknowledged Todd's grin in the mirror before turning his attention to Cassandra once more.

Shame, really, that she had such a good business head on that long slender neck. From tomorrow he could only look and admire. She was strictly off limits for anything else. But he'd enjoy the view tonight.

He saw her hands tighten on the seat rests.

"Nervous?"

The glance she gave him showed his guess to be accurate.

"Not at all."

He watched her white throat constrict briefly before she closed her eyes, allowing her glossy hair to fall forward, in a vain attempt to obscure her face.

"Tired then?"

"A little, maybe."

"A sudden change for you. New job, new life—all within hours. No-one you need to contact?"

She turned to face him once more, all sign of nerves vanished from her dark blue eyes.

"It's all sorted."

"I like a woman with no complications."

She closed her eyes once more.

In what direction had her thoughts turned? Her brow furrowed slightly, her glossily coated red lips tightened. Something had got to her and he didn't believe it was the flight.

It was the air of mystery that fascinated him. What was her background? Not the fabricated rubbish on her CV. That was just telling him what she thought he wanted to know. Why did she want the job? Again, he didn't believe a word she'd said.

With surprise he realized that he wanted to get to know the real Cassandra. It would be a novel experience. He'd usually gone out of his way *not* to know women, other than in the biblical sense. But then his interest had never been piqued on so many fronts before.

Simply two things to remember: no sex and no long-term relationship, business or otherwise.

He could do that. Perhaps.

Doubts assailed him as he watched her push her shoes off and rub her obviously aching feet together before slipping the high stilettos back into place. He frowned as he checked his response to the unconscious act.

That was the risk. He had his life on track. He didn't want anyone rocking the boat.

He chanced a look at her profile as she peered out of the window. A long curl fell forward from behind her ear, incongruously sitting at right angles to the rest of her sleek style. He smiled to himself and felt his gut tighten with attraction. Why didn't women realize that it was the imperfections that were so sexy?

He estimated that the sophisticated exterior was probably wafer thin. He wondered how long she would be able
to keep it up. It would be diverting to watch.

Depending on her ability, he'd give her six months max
to help clear the backlog of his work. It would give him time
to piece together the mysteries of her character and background and then he'd get rid of her. Everyone was expend-
able, some sooner than others. He had no long-term place in
his life for a woman.

Automatically he checked their position as they
swooped around the harbor. The Rimutaka ranges rose
darkly to their left as they changed direction, following the
curve of the coast. The city lights grew small and suddenly
vanished as they flew across the hills that enclosed Wellington. There was nothing below but the vast emptiness of
rolling hills on one side and the sea on the other. The view
by day was mesmerizing and even at night it had its charms
which Cassandra seemed to have succumbed to: the sparse
scattering of lights along the wild, windswept coastline
edging into the inkier blackness of the Cook Strait.

Cassandra could feel his eyes on her and kept hers
firmly on the light-flecked darkness below.

She hated helicopters. Always had. From the menacing
throb of their blades to the simple fact of their insignificance
when set against a vast sky. She had few physical fears. But
dangling in the air with only a flimsy metal structure
between her and certain death was one of them.

It didn't help that she was being scrutinized by a man
who didn't hide his curiosity—both intellectual and sexual.
She could deal with the intellectual. Knowing the arrogance
of the man he probably thought he'd nail her in a few short
days. He might be cold and calculating but so could she be.

It would be a close match but she would win. She had more at stake.

But, sexually? Her body responded of its own accord with a heat and suspension of wits that threatened her purpose. She wasn't here for that. She had to re-focus him, get him thinking about something that was important to him —his wealth, obviously.

"How far does your land extend?"

Her question roused him from his contemplation. He pointed north. "Out towards the Tararuas. It's really just an indulgence for me to keep such a large estate so close to the city. The real property's down south."

"Glencoe, near Shelter Springs in the Mackenzie country."

"You've done your homework."

She nodded. "Run by your brother, Callum. Your other brother, James, looks after your overseas investments in New York."

"Yep. That leaves me to do what I do best."

She couldn't resist the temptation. "Now, let's see." Her gaze held his without wavering. "According to the tabloids that's one, making money, two, making properties and three, making lov—"

"Yep, you've got the general idea."

As she turned to the window to hide her smile, she had to admit part of her was entertained by the man. But another part of her knew this whole thing would be much harder than she'd imagined. He was suspicious, picking up her lie at the interview; perceptive, sensing that all was not as it seemed with her story; and he was swift to anger, as his response to John's tirade showed.

And he was also incredibly sexy. Despite the fact that

she held him responsible for the deaths of those she most loved, just one intense look from his eyes had her body reacting like a crazy woman—someone who'd never seen a man before. All in all, he was one dangerous man.

She had to stick to her plan: bankrupt him and then get the hell out.

She smiled grimly to herself in silent satisfaction.

The agony of her hurt—her loss—could never be duplicated. But she knew how to hurt the man who was responsible for the deaths of her child and her father. There was only one thing he valued and that was his fortune. Well he wouldn't have it for much longer.

It was all she could do for them now—avenge their deaths. It was all she had left to cling to.

She closed her eyes once more.

*Don't think. Don't feel.*

*Don't think. Don't feel.*

That was her weakness. If she gave in to her feelings she would be lost.

"Are you okay?"

She snapped her eyes open and forced a smile on her face.

"Fine. Are we nearly there yet?"

"You remind me of my godson."

A real smile slipped through her defenses. God help her, humor as well. If it weren't enough to contend with his cunning and his sexuality, she also had to be subjected to his disarming humor.

"And yes we are nearly there. There's Kapiti Island below. Cliff House looks across the bay to the island."

Dallas pointed out the window to the rugged peaks of the island, a black silhouette against the darkening sky.

"It looks wild."

"It's a bird sanctuary now but has a dark history. It was Te Rauparaha's nineteenth-century stronghold: bloodshed, cannibalism, whale slaughter and the trade of women and guns, it's all ingrained in the island. But we're not on the island, its secrets are safe from us."

She had an absurd feeling that she could reach out and touch the island's darkness: find an answer to its mysteries in the shadows of her own soul.

She dragged her eyes from the brooding island and switched quickly back to the man by her side. He touched her hand with the back of his, attracting her attention to their destination that sprawled along the cliff top beneath them.

"Cliff House." They circled around once and dropped down below the house.

Heads down, they walked briskly from under the whirring blades, up towards a high brick wall that formed the rear boundary of the house. Dallas opened the door and Cassandra stepped into another world.

A rambling homestead lay before them, subtle lights illuminating its interior. Its central front was traditional—complete with verandah and fretwork—and its two wings formed elegant complements to the original.

Cassandra's gaze moved around and above the house, taking in the pin pricks of light that pierced the night sky, now the color of softest indigo. It was as if she'd walked into a painting. It was magical. She took a deep breath to steady herself. Instead, the heady mix of fragrances stirred her senses further. Even in the dim light she could see the phosphorescent white blooms of hundreds of flowers and smell their exquisite perfumes.

Instinctively she reached out and touched the jasmine

that curled around the old brick wall. Enclosed, away from the brisk sea air, the most tender flowers flourished. The brick walls were echoed in the path that meandered its way through a garden of trellised roses, tumbling clematis and flowers, hundreds of flowers—all white from the simplest of delicate blooms to the most overblown old roses, tinged with violet.

Dallas turned and waited for her to move.

"This is your garden?" She had to ask. With all her research she'd felt she'd come to know this man, this cold-hearted businessman. An all-white scented garden hadn't entered the equation at all.

"Surprised?"

"Well, just a little. It looks so—"

"Feminine? Well it is. It was my mother's. She's an Anglophile, particularly taken with the White Garden in Kent—Vita Sackville-West's. If she couldn't live in England, then England was going to come to her."

"It's stunning. I've never seen anything like it."

"Yes. Women seem to like it."

She stopped dead in her tracks. The man was insufferable.

He walked back towards her. "Insulted that I infer you're just like other women?"

"No. Simply surprised that you'd keep the garden going, given your mother lives in the South Island now. And, also, given that beauty is obviously seen by you to be a feminine thing."

"Yes, well. My mother and I are not close. But why would I do away with something that is so obviously effective with women? I like women. I like to *please* women."

"And are women pleased by your efforts?"

"Oh yes." His voice lowered further until it became

more a vibration of air against her skin, than a sound. "I make sure of it."

Suddenly he seemed too close.

"If you're trying to make me uncomfortable, you're not succeeding."

"Why would you think I was trying to do that?"

"Oh, I don't know. Perhaps testing me in some way. Seeing if I cave in under pressure."

"And do you?"

She turned to him. "I've known more pressure than you're ever likely to experience. I can do pressure. I can take whatever you throw at me."

"Really? Is that a challenge? Because I like a challenge."

"You can take it whichever way you like. I'm here to work and that's what I'll do. If you want to entertain yourself in the process, that's your prerogative."

"You know, I don't think I've ever seen eyes quite as dark a blue as yours before. They're very... inviting, especially when you're all fired up."

Was there no limit to his arrogance? He didn't even have the decency to pretend he was listening to her. "You haven't seen me anywhere near fired up."

"I look forward to it. But tell me," he continued, raising his finger to her cheek. "How come we haven't met before? Wellington is a small city."

She took a deep breath, the sudden change in tack taking her by surprise. She turned away from him sharply and began to walk away.

His hand on her arm stopped her. "You didn't answer my question."

"I like to keep a low profile."

She tried to ignore the strength contained in the touch of his hand, tried to ignore the heat that ignited a trail of fire through her veins. Long-forgotten sensations shot through her body, heating her skin and melting her resistance. She felt disoriented and suddenly found her face closer to his. Whether she'd moved closer to him, or he'd moved closer to her, she couldn't tell.

"Not any longer though. You've decided to raise the stakes in your life for some reason. With me. I wonder why?"

She swallowed. "The timing's right. I'm ready."

"I suspect..." he said, smoothing his hand along her arm. She closed her eyes briefly at how her goose-bumped skin gave away her response to his touch. When she opened them again his eyes were narrowed, but puzzled still. He knew she was responsive to him, but that was all he knew. "I suspect that you're ready in more ways than one."

"That's not what I mean."

"It might not be what you mean, but it's what you feel. Are you prepared to over-rule your feelings with your head, Cassandra?"

"I'm focused on the job. Nothing will get in the way."

"Good. Because this is a job. There will be no love affair, whatever you may want."

"I don't want a love affair," Cassandra said through gritted teeth, reining in her irritation at his arrogance.

"Really? Then you'd be unusual."

"I'm not like most women."

"What is it you want then?"

"Success."

"I hope you enjoy it when you get it, that it doesn't prove illusory." His voice was lower, softer.

Cassandra hid her confusion instantly. "I intend to."

"Come along then, your future awaits." He plucked a

single white rose and tucked it behind her ear, smoothing and pinning the recalcitrant curl into place.

He'd noticed. A hair out of place and he'd noticed. What else had he noticed? "A romantic gesture?"

"Never. I don't do romantic gestures." He leaned in towards her. "This is as romantic as I get. Tonight, a one-time only offer. A bargain—a kiss in exchange for a rose."

He brushed his lips gently against hers in a whisper of seduction, designed to tantalize. His breath quickened against her cheek as he hesitated for one long moment before pulling away.

It was as if she'd been awoken from a trance. The feel of his mouth against hers—a mere promise, a suggestion of the passion that they could have—awoke within her a heat and desire that she'd long forgotten.

But even as her trembling hand began to reach for him, as her breathing quickened and her body's responses threatened to take over, she felt a wave of icy control flow over her. She was not here for this. This had nothing to do with her plans.

She pulled away, coolly and deliberately. She *would* look him in the eye and he *would* see what she felt —nothing.

She managed it, for moments only, before turning away from him. She couldn't risk him seeing the truth, how affected she was by his touch. She heard him step away from her quickly and walk up the flight of wooden steps to the verandah and then wait.

She followed him up to the front door, having managed to recapture a few shreds of her self-possession. He stood watching her, holding open the door, while she took one last look around the garden.

It wasn't meant to have been like this. She had never

intended, never imagined, that she would feel such things. Something deep within her stirred and shifted. There was something about this place which threatened to break down her defenses. It was going to be a lot harder than she'd ever thought.

With her back to him she gently pulled the rose from behind her ear and fingered the velvety petals as she looked out across the white flowers that glowed in the dusk. She could have wept.

It was the garden of her old dreams in the days when she was truly alive, when she lived for the present, when she lived with and through her heart. It was abundant, sensual and magical, with an ethereal, dream-like quality: an other-worldliness that caught at her heart and threatened to destroy her sense of purpose.

But surely it wasn't too late? Could she really avenge her father's and Danny's death by destroying this man's wealth? She could tell him everything. She could just turn around and go back to her old life.

She turned to face him gripping another petal, too hard, and it tugged, momentarily at its base, destroying the bloom altogether before falling softly to the path in front of him.

Lights suddenly flooded out of the French windows robbing his eyes of color and exaggerating the harsh set of his lips.

"An iceberg rose destroyed by an ice-maiden, whom even a kiss could not warm."

In that instant all uncertainty vanished. She *would* live up to his assessment of her and she *would* destroy him, just as his actions had led to the deaths of those people she'd loved most in the world. She dropped the rose, white petals of innocence scattering on the brick path and walked up into the hall of the homestead, feeling the pain of her son's death with every step. It would never go away. She didn't want it to ever leave her.

The doors closed with a bang, as a freak gust of wind caught them and she turned, meeting his gaze, drawing once more on the pain to give her the strength she needed to continue.

## CHAPTER FOUR

Cassandra swept open the extravagant swags of cream curtains and looked out onto the sea—a warm cerulean blue, as smooth as silk and as lustrous—that lapped the wide semi-circular bay.

It was the same as last night, the view seemed to grab hold of her, shift her perspective, make her remember how beautiful life could be.

Even Kapiti Island—framed by sturdy trees, shaped by the wind—couldn't shift the bone-deep feeling the view gave her. The island with its bloody history looked benign in the soft sunlight of early morning. Its menacing, densely-forested ravines were brightly lit and unable to retain their sense of mystery. The savagery it had witnessed couldn't withstand the beauty of its surroundings. It was diminished, manageable.

Knowledge was a wonderful thing, thought Cassandra grimly. The more you got to know something—or someone —the less afraid you were. She just wished that were the case with Dallas Mackenzie.

She turned to look at the bedroom. With its antique silk hangings that softly draped from each of the four posts of her bed and the subtle yet elegant furnishings, it was exquisite. The embroidery in the textiles alone was stunning—cream and eau-de-Nil acanthus leaves—echoing the central ceiling rose, contrasting with the simplicity of the bare wooden floor boards and antique furniture. Beautiful.

And unexpected.

But that was Dallas Mackenzie. A man whom she thought she'd known but who was far deeper, far more complex, far more compelling than she'd given him credit for. It wasn't going to be easy. But she was in.

She pulled on her running shoes. She needed to be outside, to feel the sun on her skin and let the air clear her head. Because one thing was sure, she was going to need to keep her wits about her.

The cool spring breeze, tangy with the smell of salt and seaweed, caressed her skin gently as the sun slowly appeared over the eastern hills. She could see why Dallas stayed there. It had a compelling raw beauty which, while calming to the soul, was also challenging to the spirit. It was a special place.

The beach was no postcard-pretty scene with picturesque buildings and boats. It was clothed in rough shingle and liberally strewn with pale, sand-blasted limbs of trees that had been swept down the coast and unceremoniously dumped. The bay was encircled with lofty hills. At its outermost point, where the sun has risen, the vertical cliffs soared a hundred meters into a cloudless sky, a scrubby coating of green clinging to its rocky cover.

An invigorating, elemental place.

It was just what she needed to clear her head, to give her the strength to carry on. Because yesterday had left her feeling battered by painful and unexpected emotions.

From the desperation of wanting the job, to getting it: from the powerful attraction she'd felt for Dallas, to the hate that filled her heart when she remembered she no longer had a family, thanks to this man's incredible arrogance. But she'd done it. She'd got the job. That was the only result she needed. All she had to do now was to keep it and that meant focus, keeping a cool head and a tight rein on her emotions.

She ran straight towards a large thorn-covered branch lying in her path, and sprang right over it. As she landed, feet scrunching in the dry, coarse shingle, she smiled to herself and kept on running.


Dallas narrowed his gaze against the sun to better watch the lone figure running along the shore, ponytail swinging, waves lapping close to her feet.

He took another sip of the hot strong coffee. He needed a caffeine shot this morning. After an evening alone, mostly trying to get Cassandra out of his mind, he'd spent a restless night, trying to get her out of his dreams. And now, here she was again, in front of him.

It seemed that Cassandra was not going to give him any peace. But watching her long, tanned legs leap across a tree trunk, he thought that he could be haunted by worse things.

What was it about her? That seductive warmth barely covered by a thin veneer of ice. The urge to melt that ice and taste the heat beneath had nearly overwhelmed him last night. But his attempt to goad her into revealing herself hadn't worked. She'd frozen over even more if that were possible. And his attempt at flirtation had nearly backfired spectacularly, turning into a kiss from which he had difficulty withdrawing. He didn't want an affair. He'd told her he didn't want a love affair and yet he hadn't been able to stop himself from tasting her lips.

Crazy! She was going to drive him crazy. But she was too good at her job—and too intriguing—to let go.

He watched as her run turned into a walk and she stopped to stare at the sea.

He'd just have to throw her a curve ball every now and then in the hope of unsettling her to see what she was hiding. Yesterday, for a split second, he'd seen fear in her eyes when she'd thought things weren't going according to plan at the interview; he'd seen sadness flit across her face when she'd talked of love and he'd seen anger when John had insulted her. But what else was there?

Her mystery stirred his curiosity, her body aroused his most basic instincts, but it was her mind where the greatest attraction lay. She was going to be a challenge. It might be a business-only arrangement but he still looked forward to discovering her secrets.

He smiled to himself. He didn't fool himself it would be easy. But he wasn't after easy. He watched her—long lean limbs with curves in all the right places—and admitted she was correct to question his motives. He wanted her all right.

Dallas grimaced as he took a sip of the now cool black coffee and balanced it on the wooden railing of the deck, watching as she stopped suddenly and held her head in her hands. He stood stock still, eyes focused entirely on her. What the hell was wrong? Had she hurt herself? His instinct was to run down the path to her. He checked himself. Ridiculous. But something had got to her.

He moved towards the path, alert, ready to descend but, before he had time to get to the top of the cliff, she'd lifted her head up and turned back towards the house. He retreated to the verandah where she wouldn't notice him, set his cup on the table and snapped the newspaper open to the business pages.

What was that about? She kept more to herself than she revealed. And he really wanted to see more than she was willing to reveal. Everything.

Cassandra breathed deeply, desperate to rid herself of the steel band that threatened to tighten its grip around her head. It had come from nowhere. One minute she'd been thinking of how she could begin to put her plan for revenge into action and the next minute the memory of Danny had slipped quietly into her head, as gently and as pervasively as the waves upon the shore. The thought of him was like a kick in the guts: winding, heart-breaking. Her head tensed and she closed her eyes, willing the pain to dissipate.

He'd been just six years old—straight hair that flip-flopped into his eyes, no matter how often she trimmed it—when he'd died. She'd been trying to juggle too many responsibilities, as usual. When her father had suggested Danny go out on the yacht with him, she'd agreed, relieved to have one less responsibility to think about. The decision had haunted her every day and every night since.

She knew her father had been moodier than usual, that the business was in difficulty but she had no idea how big the problems were. She'd later learned his financial director had called while her father was out at sea to give him the news that he'd been ruined. He'd killed himself realizing he'd somehow let a multi-million dollar business that had been in his family for generations, slip through his fingers.

A single gunshot to the head was discovered when his body eventually washed to shore. Danny's body was never found. Not knowing what had subsequently happened, how Danny had disappeared, how the yacht had come to be drifting by itself, seemingly intact, had haunted her every day and every night since.

How much had he suffered? Had he watched his grand-father die and then fallen overboard himself? Had he curled up into a ball and cried her name, needing her comfort and she hadn't been there for him? Had her father taken a long time to die and Danny had to witness his pain alone? She'd never know. There was only one thing she knew. One thing she remembered in particular.

That afternoon's paper. Dallas Mackenzie's handsome face, familiar from gossip columns, under the headline, "Kiwi billionaire takes over Boston company founded in 1863". She'd known then that something had happened to her father.

She'd known he'd been on a knife edge and she'd let him take Danny. She'd joined the search teams and they'd soon located the boat. But no bodies. Not until her father's turned up, days later. As someone had turned the bloated body over, and she'd seen the effect of the gunshot wound to what was left of his face, her pain had merged with the image of Dallas's face. And only one word had come into her mind.

Revenge. Revenge upon the man whose smiling face appeared in the newspaper column while her heart lay in shreds. There would be no half-baked scenes: no demand for explanations. She knew what it was all about. Money. It was the only thing that had any value for people like that.

She'd briefly met Dallas's brother, James, but she'd refused him admittance to the funeral or a meeting afterwards. She had no interest in listening to his apologies on behalf of his brother—his company line, his superficial regret.

She cast one last look at the sea—furious for allowing its beauty to momentarily lull her into forgetting her purpose— before retracing her steps mechanically back along the shore. She was there for one reason and one reason only and the sooner she got on with the job of ruining Dallas Mackenzie, the better.

It was five minutes before she emerged from the windswept kanuka bushes at the top of the cliff—her chest heaving from the exertion—fingering a wild orchid.

"Good run?"

Cassandra turned to see Dallas, already immaculately dressed, sitting in the shadows with a cup of coffee. He slid a tall glass of orange juice across the table to her.

Her heart thudded as memories of yesterday flooded her mind and her senses. *Get a grip woman.* She hadn't expected to meet him at that hour and wished she'd been more covered up. But she didn't seem to have any choice but to join him.

"Very refreshing. Thanks for the juice."

She took a sip and sank down into a chair.

"You look as though you could do with it."

She nodded. "That path's real steep. This is just what I need." She took another long drink, enjoying the tartness of the home-made juice, and sat back. It was impossible not to feel soothed by her surroundings. "It's so beautiful here."

"That's why I stay. Beautiful and untouched. Like that wild orchid you picked."

She looked down at it and twirled it in her hands. "Someone I knew...it was his favorite flower."

She dragged her eyes away from the flower and across to where Dallas was sitting. Now wasn't the time for memories.

The sun was higher, casting the verandah, and his face, in shadow. His sunglasses hid his eyes but she could tell from the tilt of his head that he was watching her as he sipped his coffee.

Even through dark glasses he had a way of looking at her that was so intimate and powerful, she felt as if he could strip her down emotionally and physically with just one look. She looked away into the blue distance. Thank goodness she had decided to do no more than a light jog this morning. She was sweaty enough without the increase in temperature his gaze produced.

She closed her eyes, searching for a moment of calm, absorbing the heat of the sun's rays that fell onto the edge of the verandah where she sat. All she could hear was the clatter of flax and the song of wax eyes.

"It's also very peaceful," she said.

The peace was suddenly shattered by a banging door and a vibrant contralto belting out the chorus to Madam Butterfly.

Dallas raised an eyebrow. "Not always. Meet Rosa." He stood up immediately and pushed his chair back on the wooden decking. "I think I'll leave you to it."

A tall, statuesque lady threw open a side door and bustled across to them. A beaming smile shone from a face framed by a shock of steel gray hair. She was holding a large tray of breakfast things.

"*Buon giorno, bella*. Welcome, welcome. Here, I have breakfast for you both. Dallas! Where are you going? Come back here and eat something. That coffee will be no good. Oh, he's gone. He is so bad. Still, *bella*, it's very nice to meet you. I'm Rosa, Dallas's housekeeper. And if Dallas wasn't so rude he would have introduced me. But I know you. You must be the lovely Cassandra."

Cassandra blinked. She was sure that Dallas wouldn't have introduced her as such.

Smiling, Cassandra stood up to greet Rosa. She couldn't help it. The woman's warmth and humor were contagious.

"Very pleased to meet you, Rosa." Cassandra extended a hand.

Rosa laughed—a loud, raucous, infectious laugh—deposited the tea things on the table and threw her arms around her, kissing her on both cheeks.

"We don't stand on ceremony here, *bella*. Well, of course, Dallas does, but that's just him. I have to humor him sometimes. Else he tells me I have to go and we both know that I'm never going anywhere." Another loud belly laugh followed.

Cassandra grinned back, but was disconcerted. She had to adjust her ideas of Dallas, yet again, to incorporate a doting Italian mama and a home that was obviously more than a house. She could cope with a womanizing mercenary, but a doting housekeeper?

"I think Dallas had to make a call, or some such..." She trailed off, hoping she wouldn't have to spend her working life making excuses for him.

"Oh, never mind him. He's just a stroppy, impatient boy. It doesn't worry me. So you—sit down, sit down—you slept well?"

"Very well, thank you. The bed was so comfortable."

"*Perfetto.* We were not expecting anyone but we always keep a room free for visitors. Dallas is always bringing people home."

I bet he is, Cassandra thought.

"So you like the room?" Rosa continued.

"It's beautiful. And the curtains on the bed are amazing. They look like museum pieces."

"*Si.* Dallas, he chose the furnishings himself. He has good taste, eh? Silk. Very old. Dallas, he likes that sort of thing. Me, I like something machine washable, you know? But he insists. He is so artistic, just like his mother, if only he could see." Rosa shook her head. "He believes he is just like his father. And so, yes, he looks like him. And he is clever with numbers and such. But the other? No."

"The other?"

Rosa drew nearer to Cassandra, her large expressive eyes flashing with interest, while she looked around to make sure they were alone.

"The drink got Dallas's father. He was not nice to his wife, Dallas's mother." She clenched her fist and made as if to punch Cassandra. Cassandra blinked, alarmed. "Violent, you see. And my poor boy believes he will go the same way as his father because of the fight."

"Fight?" Cassandra couldn't believe how much information she was eliciting from Rosa with so little prompting. Perhaps she had nothing to fear from this woman after all.

Rosa sat back and crossed her arms awkwardly over her ample bosom, and nodded seriously. "With his brother. It was after a party and they'd all been drinking. Well you know, boys will be boys. But Dallas got angry with Callum and they fought, a bloody fight it was. But Callum, he was no innocent. He could look after himself and did too. It was bad luck for my poor boy that Callum had been at that moment using a knife. Dallas lost the top of his finger when he tried to take it from Callum. Never touched drink again. Afraid of being like his father. Same temper—perhaps." Rosa shrugged her shoulders. "But same man—never!" She sank back in her chair in a temporary reverie.

Cassandra took another sip of her tea and waited. But not for long. Suddenly Rosa sat up straight and fixed Cassandra with a fierce look.

"Dallas is *not* like his father. Even if his dear mother could not see it. But you try and tell him and he just shuts me up. Pff!! 'That's enough, Rosa. Haven't you got house-work to do, Rosa?' Anyone would think I stay here for the money! *Mica tanto!* They are my family now. Ah, well. I talk too much. So you, now. Dallas, he tell me you're here for a trial period?"

"That's right." Stunned by the abrupt change in conversation and tone, Cassandra had the feeling that a long reply wasn't required.

"It's good I think. To see if you and Dallas suit one another. That is a very good idea. It will show you what you are dealing with. All the other girls they run, run, run, when they realize what is involved."

"And what exactly would that be?"

"It's no picnic, working with a man like Dallas. Everything has to be right and he never stops. These girls, they're pretty of course, but not wanting to work so hard, if you know what I mean." She peered into Cassandra's face, as if looking for clues. "But you, you look different. Perhaps you can match him."

Cassandra heard a movement behind her. But before she could look up, Rosa leaned towards her and spoke in a stage whisper, loud enough for anyone close by to hear. "He has no patience with weakness. It won't be easy."

"Rosa! If you've quite finished trying to put off my new PA perhaps you'd be kind enough to allow her to get ready for work." He ignored Rosa's good-natured laughter and turned to Cassandra. "We're leaving in half-an-hour."

"Sure. Thanks for the tea, Rosa."

"But you haven't had any breakfast!" Rosa's laughter suddenly stopped, obviously concerned that someone would leave her household hungry.

"I'm fine, honestly."

"No wonder you are so skinny. Beautiful of course, but skinny."

Cassandra looked at Dallas helplessly in the face of Rosa's onslaught.

"Don't look at me for help. I'm in control of everything except Rosa. She's the boss here. You'd better do as she says. She takes it personally if people don't enjoy her food."

Cassandra grabbed a piece of toast. "I'll, er, take it with me."

Rosa waved her hand in reply. "You two go on now to your work. You enjoy yourselves." She withdrew, laughing loudly as she chased a prowling cat away from the kitchen door.

Cassandra caught Dallas's eye as they walked through to the hallway. "Sounds like Rosa thinks you're a kid who goes to the office to play."

"Yep. Always had a tentative hold on reality has our Rosa. Couldn't live without her though."

Cassandra cocked her head to one side in question.

"So she thinks, anyway," Dallas added hastily.

"So what time's the board meeting?"

"This afternoon. We'll be leaving for the office in half an hour." He opened a door to what looked to be his study and gave her a sweeping glance that heated her skin. "Be ready."

The door swept shut silently and Cassandra climbed the stairs to her bedroom, wondering if, despite her preparations, she would ever be ready for Dallas Mackenzie.

## CHAPTER FIVE

"Lunch is served."

Jenny, the receptionist, pushed the door open with her foot and brought a tray into the office.

"Thanks. You're a mind reader."

"Not me." She nodded in the direction of Dallas's office. "Dallas's idea. Reckoned you'd forget to eat."

"Thoughtful boss." Or, more likely, he doesn't want a weak female fainting in his office, Cassandra reasoned.

"With some people." Jenny raised an eyebrow.

Cassandra decided to ignore the innuendo and pushed away the laptop and rolled her shoulders. "Seems to be pretty thoughtful with most people, judging by the meetings we've been to this morning."

"Yeah, I'm only kidding. He's always had an eye for a beautiful PA which isn't the best criteria, if you ask my advice. But he seems to have struck lucky with you. You've made a big impression with the management team."

Jenny sat down and helped herself to a piece of sushi before sitting back and crossing her legs expectantly.

"So," she continued. "How's it going? As you expected?"

Nothing had been as she'd expected. From the obvious loyalty and affection his team showed Dallas, to the respect implicit in all his dealings with them. "There's been a few surprises."

"Such as?"

"How hands-on he is. He has a professional team supporting him, but all this"—Cassandra indicated the piles of correspondence—"detail, he does himself."

"Yeah, likes to keep an eye on everything. But it's piled up of course, since the last PA."

"What is it with Dallas and his PAs?"

"Well, the last couple have been, how can I put this politely? Oh, I can't. They've all been gold-diggers. And not so keen on doing the work, well, not the desk work."

"Ah, I get the picture."

"But if you're prepared to do the work, he's a great boss."

Cassandra helped herself to a savory. "Certainly seems to have a happy workforce."

"So you didn't expect him to be like that, huh?"

"I didn't really know what to expect." Apart from a ruthless, money-hungry bastard, thought Cassandra. "But, he seems very conscientious. The only thing my last boss was conscientious about was his golf handicap."

"Well, I don't think Dallas would know one end of a golf club from the other. He'd be more likely to swing it at someone if they annoyed him."

Cassandra laughed. "That's my impression. Direct and to the point. Not exactly worried about the niceties."

"You've got him pegged. But he *is* really good with us lot. We always come first with him. Mind you, he doesn't suffer fools gladly. His meetings with fools should be a spectator sport. Worth watching if you don't mind the sight of blood. And so long as you don't get caught in the line of fire."

"I'll make a mental note of that."

"But don't let his manner fool you. It's true he's not polite and he doesn't do small talk. Basically he can be a rude bastard sometimes. Well, most of the time actually. But he doesn't mean anything by it. It's just his way."

The door slammed closed behind them, making them both jump.

"The 'rude bastard' has just entered the room. How about putting as much effort into your job as you do your gossiping, Jen."

Jen leapt up. "Sorry, Dallas. I was just—"

"Going, I hope?"

Jen raised her eyes theatrically at Cassandra before closing the door firmly behind her. She was obviously used to such exchanges and didn't seem perturbed in the least.

"Let's make some headway with this lot." He picked up the pile of correspondence with distaste before dropping it heavily onto the desk.

"Sure." She swallowed her food hurriedly. "And thanks for the lunch."

He looked at it distractedly, having obviously forgotten he'd ordered it for her. "You haven't got time to eat. We've work to do."

Right. He was thoughtful enough to get her the lunch but his consideration obviously didn't extend to giving her time to eat it. She pushed the projects file across the desk towards him.

He sat back, put his feet on the table and plucked out a file at random.

He sighed. "This is tedious work." He pushed his hands through his hair as he flicked through the proposal with distaste.

"I've been through them and indicated whether I thought they were worth considering or not."

"Really? Ah yes, the tentative tick or cross. Brief, direct, to the point. I like it. No waffling emails to wade through first."

"Well, I thought it might give you a bit of a steer, save you reading the proposals in great depth."

"Cassandra." He put his feet back on the floor and leaned across the table. "Where have you been all my life?"

"Oh, please. Let's just get on."

He grinned as he sat back to consider the proposal.

"You're right. It's rubbish. Tell him 'no' and that his proposal is a waste of my time." He dumped the file into a clear space on the desk.

Cassandra nodded—somehow she didn't think that would go down a treat with the wealthy businessman who had made the proposal—and made a note to let him down gently.

"Next. No, wait. I can't be bothered with them. Do the same for all the ones marked 'x' and pass the ticked ones on to the legal team. They need to check them out first."

Well, that was one way to deal with a month's worth of correspondence.

"Okay. We've the HR file next." She swapped over files.

"Right. This job application. We have no jobs and even if we did I wouldn't give it to him. Tell him he's a boring bastard who doesn't deserve a job with my company."

Cassandra was beginning to see a common theme with his responses—accurate, but lacking finesse.

She made some notes for a reply to the verbose letter of

application, tactfully expressing their hope that the applicant would soon find a job more in line with his personal skills and abilities.

When it came to concerns with his own staff, Dallas took more time. He gave his complete attention to each individual letter ranging from the lowliest employee to the highest: their concerns, their dissatisfactions.

"Tell Pete he's right—I'll have the equipment checked first thing Monday—but to stop moaning and get on with it."

And so they went on, plowing their way through the mountain of correspondence with Cassandra interpreting Dallas's terse comments into a response that wouldn't alienate people. It seemed Dallas had a talent for that.

But it was the last letter of the afternoon that floored her. It was from an employee on maternity leave, thanking Dallas for paying for the care that she required during her risky pregnancy and for the toys he'd given her.

"Tell her—no, well—just say..."

For once he seemed at a loss for words.

"Shall I say that you're pleased you could help and you're glad the baby is thriving?"

He nodded. "That'll do."

Well, well. This was a new side to his character. Concern not only for his employees but a real sense of caring for a pregnant woman and her baby. Health care maybe—at a stretch—although it was unusual for someone so low in the hierarchy. But toys?

"You seem to find something amusing, Cassandra." His voice was hard and flat. Her amusement obviously rankled.

"Not really. But I just wondered..."

"Yes?"

"Were they fluffy toys? Bears, pandas? That sort of thing?"

He shot her a warning glance and stood up.

"Soft, cuddly...?" She let her voice trail off as she looked up innocently into his face. He leaned over the desk, his hands planted firmly either side of her.

"Soft, cuddly"—his low tones turned husky as if he were uttering endearments to her—"innocent. They're all things I appreciate, in others, in their place. But don't ever mistake me for being these things. There is no place in my life for them. My taste runs hotter than that." His eyes flicked to her lips before arresting her gaze once more.

His roughened voice and hot gaze bypassed her defenses and triggered a surge of corresponding heat within her. The barriers were down and instinct made her want to keep them down.

"More passionate, perhaps?"

She saw him waver, could sense the struggle between responding to her flirtation and replacing the barrier of professionalism between them. She licked her lips, held his gaze and waited.

He reached over to her, gripped her chin with his fingers, "Don't mess with me unless you're prepared for the consequences, Cassandra."

A blaze of need gnawed in her gut. She knew what he was talking about and it wasn't business.

"I have no intention of doing anything other than work for you."

He smiled grimly and released her chin. "Good. So we're both in agreement—for now. But if you change your mind, let me know. I might be interested."

Cassandra pressed her eyelids closed with her fingers, astounded by the arrogance of the man. She opened them to find his face closer, his eyes focused on her mouth, his lips near hers. She felt disoriented by his closeness.

"Well, perhaps not as disinterested as you appear, eh?" His eyes were cool and arrogant.

His tone effectively snapped her back to reality. "I am not some easily impressed young virgin to seduce—"

"Cassandra. I have no illusions on that score. I have safely assumed you left your softer side behind years ago, if you ever had one. And that's fine because my interest in things soft and cuddly apply only to other people's children."

The shock slammed in her gut as his words hit home in a way that he could never have imagined. He was right. That part of her was long gone, lost with her son. She pushed her chair back abruptly and rose to meet him eye to eye.

"We're two of a kind then. A perfect business arrangement."

"We'll see about that. You've got a week to prove yourself to me remember."

"That's all I'll need." *I can ruin you in a week, no sweat.*

When she turned she saw his sharp gaze upon her. She swallowed down the panic as she realized something in her tone must have revealed the *double entendre* of her words.

"Um, one week. I can't help feeling it will be an interesting one."

It was only after he'd swung the door closed behind him that she exhaled shakily. She had to be careful.

———

Cassandra ate alone.

She'd accompanied Dallas back in the helicopter but might just as well have been alone for all the conversation they'd had. He definitely seemed to be avoiding engaging with her at any level.

She didn't need his attentions, she told herself firmly. Not for what she wanted to do with him. But even as she told herself this, she sat back, pushed her unfinished dinner to one side and sighed.

To say she was confused was an understatement. She was clear what she wanted. She wanted to ruin Dallas Mackenzie; she wanted to make him pay for her son's and her father's deaths. But what she wasn't clear about was why her body reacted to him without engaging her brain. Why his accidental touch burned through her clothes, torching her skin and conjured images of their bodies moving together, slickly, intimately.

She shook her head in an effort to banish the unwanted images and then rose and backed out of the room, taking the plates back to the kitchen.

Dallas had been avoiding Cassandra all evening.

He'd eaten alone and he'd stayed away with the sole intention of making sure he didn't stray from the original agreement with her.

It was business, not pleasure.

But it had been a pleasure to see how her elegant hands moved across the laptop, gentle, yet in control and how she walked—upright, lithe—the walk of a dancer.

But it *must* be about business. And her manner was perfect with his team: professional, but slightly aloof.

Except when she'd teased him about the toys he'd given to Emma's baby. That lapse had nearly undone him. The smile shining in her dark blue eyes—the color of the sea after the sun has slipped beyond the horizon—taunting him to respond. And he damn near had.

Yep, a professional relationship it had to be. And it could be. Hadn't he learned to curb his own feelings in the interests of business? Hadn't he learned that he would never be able to marry or have children? The risk of repeating his father's history was too great. He was his image: physically he was the same, large and strong; emotionally the same, swift to anger and physiologically he was the same, allergic to alcohol. The writing was on the wall and he'd read it.

Despite what Rosa hoped, there would be no marriage, no commitment for him. And so far he'd managed it. As soon as women discovered he would never marry, they were off. As soon as he discovered a woman hoped to change him, he was off.

Then why, since he'd met Cassandra, had he been unable to control his own thoughts and feelings? He wasn't some adolescent boy. But it was no good avoiding the situation. He'd confront her, show her they could work together without letting their instincts take control. Anything to ease the frustration.

Immersed in his own thoughts, Dallas hadn't seen the door begin to open until he collided with Cassandra. He grabbed her in time to stop her from falling, but the dishes went flying, skittering across the polished floor. Broken dishes and food were scattered everywhere.

But it was the effect of her warm body close to his that scattered his own thoughts and the intentions that he'd just spent the past few hours trying to stick to.

"Leave it."

"I was taking it to Rosa."

"Leave it. Someone else can clear it up. I want to talk to you."

All thoughts of keeping a professional distance from her had fled when their bodies had collided. He wanted to feel her lips against his, he wanted to stir the passion he sensed within her.

"But, the dishes—Rosa..."

"Rosa's left early for the week-end."

"So we're alone."

Dallas could hear the huskiness of desire creep into her low voice and it led to an unalterable decision on his part. This felt too important, too out of control, to stop.

"You uncomfortable with that?"

She shook her head but before she could say anything further, Dallas bridged the gap between them and slid his fingers into her long, glossy hair. He held her head in his hands and tilted her face to his, searching her expression for resistance but, finding none, he tightened his grip and pulled her towards him. His mouth sought hers, hungrily intent on satisfying the need that had been growing all day.

He tensed as he felt her initial jolt of surprise. But the unformed sound in her throat turned into a breathless gasp that dissolved into his mouth as she relaxed in his arms. He slid his hands around her back, pulling her to him, needing her to be tight against him.

Cassandra should have moved. She should have pulled away when Dallas had hesitated and searched her face, as if for permission to continue. But she hadn't, and he'd correctly taken that as his answer and now his grip around her was complete. She had nowhere to move, nor did she want to.

She was unprepared and running on instinct alone—an instinct that responded at a basic level to the domination of his mouth over hers, igniting a passion which there was no subduing.

He moved his hand slowly and firmly down her back, pressing her closer to him, forcing her to succumb to his power. But the blaze of passion his kiss ignited demanded her own satisfaction and she met his force with her own, her tongue entwining sensually and strongly with his, resisting surrender and challenging his domination. He groaned deeply in response and the last shreds of coherent thought fled as passion—unadulterated and raw—overtook her.

She slipped her hands around him and drove her hands up under his shirt, fanning her fingers over his heated skin, desperate to feel the contours of his body: its muscles, sinews and skin moving under her touch as his own hands moved under her top, echoing her exploration with one of his own.

As his hands swept up her hips, she gasped and pulled away from his lips, allowing his mouth access to her jaw, her neck and lower. She closed her eyes under the sensory over-load of his warm lips against her throat and his finger nails as they raked down her back.

It was as if a switch had been flicked, destroying in one fell move all her composure and guard, making her forget everything except the fire that ran through her body, every-thing except the anticipation of where his fingers and tongue would go next.

It was as if she were teetering on the edge of an abyss of ecstasy, wanting to fall, desperately wanting to descend with him into oblivion.

But the oblivion didn't come.

He pulled away suddenly. Bereft and needy she

sought his lips out once more with her own, but he pulled back, breathless, his dark impassioned eyes full of her, only her.

"Cassandra, are you sure?"

It was all that it took. One moment of hesitation, one moment for her thoughts to take control.

*What on earth was she doing?*

She pulled away slowly and looked down at her shirt that hung open. She didn't remember him undoing the buttons, she remembered nothing but the feel of his skin against hers, his breath against her body, his hands stirring a passion she'd long-presumed dead. While her heart still hammered, it was from another emotion now.

*Humiliation.*

She'd just shown him that he'd been correct all along. She was just like the other PAs. But more than that, she was shocked at how easily she was able to betray her son.

A shutter came down in her heart.

"No, I'm not sure. I'm sorry, but I can't do this."

She could hear the icy edge to her tone and could see its effect in Dallas's eyes.

His arms slipped slowly off her, the old cold, hard expression fell back into place, sealing over the raw, open passion of only moments before. He stepped away with a brief nod.

"Right." He thrust his hands in his pockets as if he didn't trust them. "Right," he said again. "Just to clarify. We can still work together if we sleep together. The two are not mutually exclusive."

She shook her head. "It's not possible."

He cocked his head to one side. "I think it is."

She shook her head again.

"Why? Because I don't think you're immune to me."

She bit her lip. There was nothing she could say without telling him the truth, and that must never happen.

He gave an exasperated sigh and walked to the drinks cabinet where he hesitated, as if suddenly aware he was about to pour a drink. "Look, I'm sorry. I'll get us a coffee. We need to talk."

She nodded. If she was to work with him she couldn't run away now. She had to face him, get it over with, get out of the mess she'd created somehow and then resume her plan.

As he walked out to the kitchen to get them coffee, she sat down and took a deep, unsteady breath.

She had to do better than that. For goodness sake, she wasn't some inexperienced teenager. She'd nearly undone all her work. For what? A brief fling with the boss?

But even as her mind formulated the thought, her memory taunted her with the heat of his lips searing her neck and of his hips pressed against hers. It would be more than a brief sexual encounter. She knew it, deep down. But that only made it worse.

*She would be betraying her son and her father! The two men who meant the most in the world to her.*

He was responsible for their deaths, she reminded herself. But nothing she'd seen or learned about him fitted the profile that she'd been clinging to. Nothing. What if she had been wrong? The thought floored her.

*What if she had been wrong?* The thought would not go away.

He touched her arm. Electrified, she looked up and met his gaze.

"Your coffee."

He sat opposite her and from his expression she knew

he wasn't going to make it easy for her. Why didn't he take his eyes off her?

She took a sip of her coffee, looking up at him over the rim of the cup. He was watching her lips. She shivered and sat back, willing herself to be relaxed but on guard. How could she be this contradiction?

"Why are you here, Cassandra?"

If there was one thing about Dallas, it was that you never knew what he was going to say next.

"To work, of course."

"I knew you weren't like other women when I first saw you."

Despite her confusion, a bubble of laughter surfaced from nowhere. "All the other women, they—"

"Want to screw me, of course—either physically or financially. It often amounts to the same. But you? I think we can safely rule out you wanting to screw me now. And, as for being my PA, there's an intensity in you that makes me question your motives. You're not here for that either, are you?"

"Of course I am. Why else do you think I'm here?"

"I don't know."

He leaned forward and ran his hand along her bare arm, trailing his nails against her flesh. She drew in a breath sharply as her body reacted of its own volition. "Don't."

"Why not?"

"I'm your PA, not your—not anything else. You didn't mention this in the ad."

"It's not required. And it's not something I've ever done before, if you must know." He slid his hand along to her wrist and held it, his thumb rubbing inside her palm.

For some reason there seemed a direct line to more intimate parts of her body. She jerked away. "It's a professional relationship. Nothing more."

"Who's to say it can't be both?"

"I say."

He dropped her hand suddenly. "It's up to you. If you don't want to pursue it, then we won't."

"But my job?"

He stood up and strode to the windows, staring out at the dark night. "Do you really think I'd dismiss you because you won't sleep with me? Give me some credit. You're just the sort of PA I've been wanting, *needing*, for years."

Guilt swept through her. What was she doing? How had she ever turned herself into a woman prepared to deceive and ruin a man for revenge? And not just any man, but this man whose one look melted her, making her forget everything, except the need to feed the growing hunger.

She rose. She had to be strong; she knew he'd despise anything else. As she approached him, she hardly knew what she was going to do and she could see the answering tension in his face.

She dragged her gaze up from his lips to meet his eyes, now unreadable, guarded. She paused, feeling almost consumed by the throbbing pulse of anticipation and need, her body screaming out for satisfaction. Just one step and she could satisfy it. The breath caught in her throat, encapsulating her inner struggle and just one word came to her mind.

*Danny.*

"I'll be your PA, but nothing more."

"That's fine." He said, too hastily.

"Look—"

"Go to bed, Cassandra. Go now." It was no kind-hearted suggestion. It was a command to be instantly obeyed.

"Good night then."

She hesitated, waiting to hear him wish her "good-night", not wanting to leave it like this. But there was no response. His body, his face and his eyes were all quite cold. He'd cut her off completely.

"Right." She turned slowly away from him. "Right," she repeated as she walked to the door.

This is what she wanted, she thought to herself desperately, her brows knitting and tears threatening now that he couldn't see her. Then why did it feel the opposite?

# CHAPTER SIX

He *would* have her. He'd worked off some of the frustration in the gym. But he still had a consuming need for Cassandra.

He knew she'd be expecting business as usual. The cold anger that had consumed him the previous evening had gone, leaving him in control once more. He was calling the shots and he'd play her just as she was playing him. He knew she'd be expecting him to be cool and professional. Well he wasn't in the mood for providing the expected. He wanted her and she'd know it.

He flung open the door to reception. "Where's Cassandra?"

"She's in a meeting, she—"

"I want her here, now, before my 9 o'clock meeting. Jen! When I say 'now', I don't mean after you've finished checking your phone messages."

He closed the door and leaned briefly against it. He *would* have her.

· · ·

Cassandra strode into his office with a confidence she didn't feel. She wished he'd stop staring at her. This was going to be harder than she'd thought.

"I've brought the Stewart file."

His gaze had a heat that threw her. Surely he'd agreed that their relationship was to be purely professional? And why didn't he speak?

"John Stewart and his proposal to invest through him in Knight Enterprises," she elaborated to fill the silence.

He nodded and leaned back in his chair, his stare intense and intimate.

"Thank you for that clarification. I know who he is. Any further gems to add to the pre-meeting brief?"

Oh, boy, this was going to be tough. She smiled coolly. The bastard was not going to get away with this.

"Actually yes, quite a lot."

He leaned further back in the chair, challenging her with his arrogant stance and with his unrelenting gaze. "Can't wait to hear it."

It was a challenge she'd meet though. He was making it clear that, while he was angry, he still wanted her. And the worst of it was that it was reciprocal. She wanted him as badly. Or rather, her body did. But she was determined that her mind would win over her traitorous body. It had to. Or else it would have all have been for nothing.

She had to make it equally clear that there was no way she would have sex with Dallas Mackenzie. And what better way to begin than to give him some bad news.

"Then I'll begin." She flicked open her laptop. "Knight Properties is a good solid family business. But—" She made the mistake of looking up at him, caught momentarily by his steely gaze, arrested by the sight of his fingers tapping a pen. She swallowed.

His eyes softened slightly, a smile hovering around his lips. "But what? Why are you so against this proposition, Cassandra?"

For a moment, swayed by the way his eyes bored into hers, Cassandra thought he was talking about a different proposition.

However, unlike her, whatever he was thinking was controlled. His attention was all on the business. "My management team has okayed it," he continued, relentless in his focus.

She looked back down at her laptop. It was the only way she could concentrate. "It's not about the business. That's great. It's a good solid business and the family who own it are happy to have others join them. They need an injection of capital to see them over some major refurbishment work on one of their office blocks. But it will come right and it could be an excellent investment."

"So. Cassandra." It wasn't the two words that disturbed her—although each was spoken as if it were a complete sentence containing complex meaning—but the tone he used. Suggestive. Loaded with intent.

He stood up suddenly and walked behind her. She froze at the feel of his touch on her shoulders, his hand on hers as he removed her fingers from the laptop keys. Bending over, he brought his cheek alongside hers as he flicked open a new web page. He didn't move for several seconds, obviously aware of the effect his presence was having on her, and wanting to prolong it. But, as a smile flickered on his lips, he slowly withdrew and returned to his seat.

"Are you all right Cassandra? You look a little flushed."

She glared at him, ignoring his question. "This is Knight's website."

"Well spotted. Explain further why I shouldn't invest. If the figures stack up, I want in. You know I can recognize a good thing when I see it."

Cassandra swallowed hard and refused to meet his eyes as he sat back down at his desk. Instead, she switched pointlessly between programs on her laptop. "Because I suspect that John wants to strip the company of its assets and use them in some of his other businesses that are by no means as sound as this one."

"It's not unheard of. Nothing new. We'll be repaid handsomely for our investment."

"But the family who own it know nothing about these plans. They are simply seeking an investment partner to see them through a tricky patch. They're resigned to knowing it'll be for the long term, but to asset strip? They have no idea."

"Mackenzie Investments is about making money, Cassandra. It's not about making friends; it's not about holding people's hands as they flounder through their business lives. If they can't deal with it, they need to get out."

Incensed at his lack of feeling, all thought of her own discomfort was forgotten. "Dallas, it's your company and your decision. I'm just advising you that it's unethical."

He raised an eyebrow. "Strong words. Is that how you see me? Unethical?"

"It's what you call someone who destroys people's lives just because they can." She turned away, only to turn back, her eyes blazing. "For goodness sake, you've no right to destroy someone just because you can. There are people's lives at stake here. You can't ride rough shod over people. Not even the smallest child." She took a deep breath, trying desperately to calm herself. She could see Dallas had registered her extreme response, had noticed that her arguments had veered to the personal.

"What's this really about, Cassandra?"

She tried to backtrack. "Assuming you did invest, assuming that the deal went ahead. After, I estimate, two years you'd have bled the company dry of money, you'd withdraw your support, sell it on. And then what? Who would want to deal with you again? What price your reputation?"

There was a long pause during which neither moved, just held each other's gaze. It was Cassandra who turned away first, unable to match Dallas's willpower.

"Must be time for my meeting. Send in John on your way out."

Cassandra hated being dismissed but rose and left the office without a backward glance, inwardly railing at his imperious commands.

"John." Cassandra nodded and held out her hand. But he didn't rise out of his seat and he didn't shake her hand. "Dallas is ready for you now." She indicated the open door.

"Dallas seen some sense? Sending you on your way before our meeting?" He shook his head. He rose to his feet and dipped his head to hers. She tried not to recoil. "Here's a tip, leave the business to the men."

She stepped back, trying hard not to respond, and watched as he walked with a swagger into Dallas's office, his too-loud greeting striking a false note that betrayed his nervousness.

Alone in her office, Cassandra sank back into her chair and wondered what she had to do to get through to Dallas. She had no idea how this meeting was going to proceed. Dallas appeared to favor investing against her recommendation. It fitted her previous image of him. Single-minded pursuit of a goal: money. But it didn't fit the image of the man she was getting to know. Which was the correct image? She reckoned she'd only know for sure when she saw him using his funds to back someone—when he returned from the meeting and dumped an untidy bundle of papers on her desk and barked an instruction. Until then, she had to wait.

She didn't have to wait long. She'd just dropped some mail off at reception when John came bursting out with Dallas following close behind, his brow lowered into a frown.

John stopped abruptly in front of her. "It was you, wasn't it? Christ, what do you know other than how to wear a dress well?"

"Stop right there, John. I've warned you when we last met. I'm with Cassandra on this one. It's not a deal."

Cassandra's gaze snapped up to Dallas. She could see he was angry but only from his utter coldness and control.

"So much for loyalty then, eh Dallas? You remember the fights I've got you out of? Remember them? Remember the parties, the women, the drink? You were a better man then. At least you were your own man, not being used by a woman but too besotted to see it."

Dallas's face was pale with fury and Cassandra reached out and placed her hand on his arm. She had to stop him before he lost control like he did at the party.

"Dallas?"

A muscle in his jaw twitched, as her voice and touch registered with him, as control smoothed over the anger.

"John." Dallas's voice was suddenly weary. "Business is business. I'll always be here if you need me but I'm going to let this one go. It's not my line of work."

"Since when?"

Dallas cast a brief glance at Cassandra.

"Since now."

John shook his head, his face haggard and eyes bloodshot. He walked out of the office without looking back.

"I take it you didn't invest then?" Cassandra's tone was intentionally light.

He grinned. "You take it right." He sighed. "Come in to my office."

Cassandra followed him in and sat down.

"I'm sorry, Dallas. John's your friend and he looked pretty desperate. I guess this was make or break with him?"

Dallas nodded. "John will be all right. He's an old friend. I owe him, but not that much. I may be loyal but I never compromise on some things. And that's principally honesty. And John wasn't honest with me or the investment company. Honesty is important to me, Cassandra. Best to remember that."

She nodded jerkily, trying to think of something to fill the lengthening silence and failing. Dallas gaze narrowed as he sensed her discomfort.

"You okay?"

"Yes." Cassandra exhaled the word through barely open lips and rose, needing to move, needing to break the tension. She walked over to the window that looked across the city, towers shining in the morning mist, and across the harbor. She felt as if the world had shifted beneath her feet and there had been no earthquake to explain the phenomenon. Only Dallas, behaving like a decent man. "So what made you change your mind?"

A slow smile curled on his lips. "Something tells me you've not checked your emails recently." He turned his laptop to face her.

She shook her head in confusion and walked over to it,

quickly logging in to her emails. "No, I've been busy, I—" She stopped talking as she saw an email from him sent over an hour before. She swiftly read it and turned back to him, arms folded, lips pursed.

"So you'd already made up your mind when you saw me? You'd actually met up with Knights and made your decision."

"That's right."

"So why did you let me go on?"

"I like watching you get agitated."

Cassandra could feel the blush rising. "You've been playing with me."

He slipped forward on the edge of his seat so he was close to her. "Not as much as I'd like to."

She closed her eyes in a vain attempt to stem the rise of desire. It didn't.

"I've expected a lot from you today," he continued, as if his comment hadn't been heavy with sexual innuendo. "If you're interested, I've been more than satisfied with your performance. We've a week-end ahead of us. Less work, a little fun. You want to continue?"

She turned to face him and they were so close she could see the different shades that made up the gray of his eyes: eyes that looked much warmer than before.

"Yes, I do. It's what I want."

He nodded. "I hoped you'd say that. I've confirmed your security access and HR will be in touch over the other standard issues."

"Thank you." Her eyes flitted across his face before resting on his lips, drawn close together. "So..." She couldn't help licking her lips. "This 'fun' you have in mind. I thought you were a 24/7 workaholic."

His lips curved into a smile that sent shivers through her

body. "Depends on who I'm with." She wanted him to step forward, to bridge the slight gap between them but he returned to his desk. "I'll see you later."

He should be thanking *her*, he thought, as he watched her leave the room.

He sighed as the door clicked shut, ran his fingers through his hair and sat down at his desk once more, checking through his emails mechanically.

Despite the ticking off—which he had to admit he deserved—he was grateful to her. She was right about engaging emotionally with people. It wasn't purely a matter of honesty or economics that had helped him make his decision. It had been a meeting that he'd had, at Cassandra's urging, with the family seeking investment. It had made it personal. Something he'd shied away from for more years than he could remember. And it had felt right.

That was something that he would always thank Cassandra for: her honesty in making him see a better way. However, it still didn't mean that he would emotionally engage with people in his personal life. Marriage and children weren't for him and never would be. His baser impulses—the ones inherited from his father—saw to that. And those impulses were still there in plenty. He could have hurt John if Cassandra hadn't stopped him.

He closed his eyes and leaned back in the chair at the memory of her touch on his arm. So light and yet so powerful. How did she do it? Her voice calling his name had come to him as if through a red haze and then, at her touch, he'd felt the anger recede.

The connection he had with her was like nothing he'd

experienced before and he felt compelled to pursue her, if only to get her out of his mind, out of his senses. Of course, it wouldn't go beyond the physical, he'd make sure of that. There would be no long-term future to it.

He snapped the laptop closed and turned out the light. This weekend. He'd pursue her, and he'd get her, this weekend.

Cassandra climbed into bed that night and lay, exhausted, looking out of the window at the dark clouds scudding across the lighter colored sky.

She'd done it. She'd got past security and could access the real data. But at what cost? She was emotionally drained. The business with John had opened up the raw wound of Danny's death and she'd had trouble containing her feelings. But she'd done it. Just in time, she'd managed to pull back and control her grief.

She'd built up the trust she needed to exact revenge. But she'd also drawn closer to Dallas than she'd intended. She'd made him open his mind to these people: to build on his belief of honest trading and make him see that he was dealing with real people, with real people's lives. His willingness to do as she'd suggested and actually meet with the family had astounded her.

It didn't fit with his arrogance. It didn't fit with his "profits at any cost" reputation. It didn't fit with her perceptions of him.

What if she were wrong? But how could she be? She'd been there. She'd seen the papers. Everything pointed to him being behind the takeover of her family's company.

But that still didn't stop her dreams being invaded by the feeling of his mouth against hers, of his voice whispering her name in the dark, of his hand reaching for her and finding her.

# CHAPTER SEVEN

Grapevines raked the valley leading the eye up to a sprawling pantiled villa set amidst an olive grove. Beyond, in the distance, an azure blue sea marked the property's boundary from which green hills rolled in waves towards them like a rumpled carpet. Cassandra couldn't get used to the landscape, produced by seismic activity rather than the slow erosion of weather and water. It was dangerous, unpredictable.

The helicopter descended suddenly, leaving the sea behind and enclosing them in the twisted woody vines and fresh green leaves of the vineyard. The sun dazzled Cassandra's eyes as they circled around the multileveled villa, from under which thatched loggias jutted onto a long terrace that abutted a sparkling swimming pool, alive with the splashes of children. It was scene straight out of the French Riviera, except Onihau was on the other side of the world.

Sweeping lawns, crisscrossed with a network of paved walks and gardens, spread beneath them as they followed a drive lined with sleekly expensive cars. They came to rest at the helipad at the rear of the house.

"Ready?" Dallas jumped out and held the door open for her. Cassandra leaped out nimbly, thanking heaven that she'd chosen flat sandals. Her dress flapped in the wind as they walked towards the deck where two people emerged from a small group to meet them.

"Cassandra, I'd like you to meet Guy and Lucia—my oldest friends."

A ruggedly handsome man and an exotically beautiful woman, greeted Cassandra with wide smiles and a warmth that surprised and unnerved her.

Meeting Dallas's friends was going to be interesting. Another set of pieces to add to the Dallas puzzle. Perhaps here, away from work, she'd find confirmation of her earlier assumptions about the man. Because everything else she'd seen so far contradicted them.

She extended her hand to greet Guy who pulled her to him and kissed her on both cheeks. "Lovely to meet you Cassandra. About time Dallas got himself sorted. He's his own worst enemy when it comes to pleasure."

"Work actually, Guy. Cassandra Lee is my new PA. Thought I'd introduce her to some of the crowd so she knows her way around the business, and my life." He cast a narrow-eyed glance at Cassandra.

He was up to something. Another test of some sort?

"Welcome Cassandra. Drink? Usual for you Dallas?" Lucia also kissed both Dallas and Cassandra.

She had warm brown eyes that sparkled with humor. Cassandra instantly liked her and felt herself relax. It had been a long time since she'd felt a connection with a woman. Her life had been consumed by work and, latterly, grief, for so long that she'd almost didn't recognize the flutter of spirits that stirred within for what it was—lightheartedness. It felt good. Perhaps she might enjoy herself here after all.

"Heard about your post-meeting meeting with John yesterday. He phoned. After all that, you actually invested some funds in him. Bit rash wasn't it?" Lucia smiled affectionately at Dallas.

He looked briefly at Cassandra. "Not really. His strengths were always on the production side. I've shares in a small company he'd suit. It gives him the opportunity to return to management but without the risks. Should be a steady earner and keep him out of trouble."

Lucia laughed. "But not his beautiful wife, I should imagine. Running a small production unit in rural New South Wales won't be her idea of fun."

"Well in that case, he's best off without her."

Lucia turned to Cassandra, laughing. "Meet Dallas, the man of conscience. Though perhaps not the man of chivalry."

"I couldn't possibly comment." Cassandra grinned.

As Guy handed out the drinks, Lucia steered Cassandra towards the house. "So, Cassandra, welcome. How come you're involved with Dallas?"

"It's interesting work and I needed a job."

"Interested in Dallas?"

Cassandra stopped, mid-stride, surprised by the woman's candor.

"Don't look so surprised. Dallas has been through so many PAs that it's become a bit of a joke. I mean, he's handsome, intelligent"—she looked at him over her dark glasses—"and as sexy as hell. And yes, Dallas and I have had our moments—before I met Guy, that is. No hard feelings on either side. Dallas and I weren't in love. And I am, very much in love with Guy."

"I can see that. And no, I'm here to do a job. That's all. I have no designs on Dallas."

Lucia looked at Cassandra searchingly. "Maybe it's as you say." She smiled. "We'll see. Just take care of him—in a professional capacity of course—he needs it."

"I think Dallas can look after himself."

Again, Cassandra was caught off guard by the woman's shrewd expression. "We can all care for ourselves, but sometimes life's a little better if you can ease someone's burden."

"And Dallas's burden would be?"

"You'll have to work that out for yourself. And, hopefully, in the process, Dallas can help you."

"I'm perfectly fine thank you. I don't need help from anyone."

Lucia drew close and Cassandra could see the beautiful eyes held a trace of suffering in their depths. "Just by virtue of the fact that you say that indicates that you probably do." She smiled and linked arms with Cassandra before she could remonstrate and turned towards the main party, where groups of people chatted. "Come on, let me introduce you to the others."


Dallas watched Lucia and Cassandra chatting and laughing together, their body language revealing their enjoyment in each other's company. He smiled. It was good to see Cassandra enjoying herself, joking and smiling. And Lucia would be good for her.

He watched Lucia for a few moments remembering how, long ago, they'd been lovers. It had been difficult finishing their relationship at the time—she was a wonderful woman. And, thank goodness, one of his closest friends now. But he knew she had needed more than he could give.

Introducing her to Guy was the best thing he could have done for her and she'd eventually come to understand he was right. They were perfect for each other and, after a rocky start, their relationship had proved to be everything she needed. Guy could give her the love that he couldn't. Love just wasn't his thing and never would be.

His eyes strayed once more to Cassandra. But with Cassandra, there was no such talk of love and children. Perhaps he needed to make absolutely sure. But one thing he was sure of—he wanted her. And watching her now only made his need greater.

The white dress set off the honeyed tones of her new tan exquisitely; its soft lines barely grazed her curves but had you thinking about them, all the same. There was little on show—simple round neck, bare arms, mid length—but she looked cool, comfortable and extremely sexy. She stood tall and confident, her hair falling like a cloud-shadowed waterfall down her back. He couldn't help but watch her. And he wasn't the only one. Admiring, curious looks followed her. But she appeared completely oblivious, enjoying herself with Lucia.

A woman of mystery. But not for much longer, he hoped.

He'd set Todd the task of finding out her background today. In the meantime he'd brought her here, to where a wide range of people would be gathering, to see if anyone knew her. But they didn't or they weren't saying. It would be interesting to discover what this elegant beauty was hiding. Because she was sure hiding something.

He watched as Lucia was drawn away by another guest and Cassandra joined a small group of women, some of whom he recognized. From looking relaxed and at ease, she stiffened slightly and the smile froze a little. He'd had experience of a few of the women at various parties to know why Cassandra would be feeling uncomfortable. She'd be like a fish out of water with them.

"Honestly, darling," the dyed-blonde said in an exaggerated whisper. "He's fantastic in bed. Positions I've only read about. He was up for it—literally."

The other women hooted with laughter while Cassandra gripped her glass, smiled, and tried to control an urge to run.

The women's talk of sex, TV, clothes and gossip about more sex, was completely normal no doubt but a million miles from the concerns that kept her awake at night. It was a comfort of sorts to know that normal life went on elsewhere. It didn't make it any easier though. She still felt as if she'd descended from another planet. They were friendly enough, if not a little curious and wary. Quick glances in her direction, and at each other, showed an undercurrent to the conversation from which she was excluded. It was fine by her. She hadn't heard talk like this since college.

The recounting of sexual exploits continued as she tuned out and looked around her. No sign of Dallas. She sighed. The sooner this whole business was over the better. And the sooner she got away from this group the better. She'd listened to them long enough for politeness's sake. She'd seek out the kids by the pool rather than put up with their inane conversation any longer.

She downed her glass and turned to walk away.

"So, Cassandra." One of the women turned to her. "You're with Dallas then?"

"Yes. I'm his PA."

"But, you're like, with him, right?"

"Yes. In a purely professional capacity."

The others laughed as if she'd made a joke.

"No, really." What was wrong with them?

The woman who'd spoken to her touched her on the arm. "It's okay. We've all lusted after him. Tell me, what's he like in the sack?"

A few of the other women giggled but a hush descended.

"Come on, we'd love to know."

"I work for the man, I don't sleep with him."

"Looking like you do? I don't think so, do you girls?"

"What? I look like a slut?"

The woman laughed uncertainly. It was finally dawning on her that Cassandra might not share the same interests as the rest of the group and that she was getting angrier by the minute.

"You can tell us," whispered another woman who hadn't picked up on Cassandra's irritation yet.

"Sorry, I was just going—oh, over there."

She tried to move but the other woman put one firm hand on her arm. "Spill the beans and then we'll let you go."

Christ, what did it take? Her temper snapped.

"Well, yep, you're right. What can I say? I've had sex with Dallas Mackenzie and he's great."

Her response was met with stunned, gaping-mouthed silence as the group of women looked over her head, behind her.

"Darling! Giving away all our secrets? Excuse me ladies." Dallas grabbed her elbow and drew her away from the wide-eyed group.

"Cassandra! I leave you for five minutes and you end up frightening the natives."

"Well, at least I've given them something to talk about."

He grinned. "And the publicity will do me no harm."

"Hey, I'm sorry, but I'm not used to that kind of talk."

"No problem. You don't have to apologize. I quite liked the dirty talk, myself."

"Stop teasing, Dallas." She tried to poke him in the ribs but he grabbed her finger before she made contact and twisted her hand around into his.

"Come on, let's get away from these people for a while."

"Good idea."

He led her out to the pool where children continued to splash—alone now that the sun was hotter and their parents had retreated inside.

"I'll get you a drink, won't be a minute."

Cassandra glanced over at the children. All eight were together, playing some game to do with mermaids and dolphins. The youngest boy was encircled by a float and was happily paddling his way across from the shallow end, following a ball. The children had been part of the reason she hadn't yet retreated inside, out of the brilliant sunshine. She wanted to keep half an eye on them. Since Danny's death she'd found it difficult to be around kids. Drawn to them, but at the same time afraid of the effect they'd have on her. Her proximity to them now sobered her mood.

Dallas handed her a glass of wine.

"You like children?"

"Of course." She felt cool, detached. The light-hearted-ness of minutes before, now forgotten.

"You want children some day?"

Cassandra looked away and took a deep, steadying breath. "Yes. Who doesn't?"

Don't go near the truth. Don't allow him to lead you there.

"Me, for one."

"Why on earth not?"

"A number of reasons, personal reasons. But it's not for me. No marriage, no children."

Suddenly it clicked. "You're trying to warn me off, aren't you? You still think, despite everything I've said, that I want to sleep with you, marry you and have your babies. Well, let me tell you, you couldn't be further from the truth."

He caught her hand and she caught her breath. He leaned down and kissed her completely, confidently, persuasively on the mouth. She should pull away. She should... Instead she relaxed under the command of his lips, stirred by the touch of his tongue on hers. As the kiss deepened her body swayed into his and a wave of heat surged through her body.

But then he stopped, pulled away, leaving her breathless and bereft.

As the warmth and power moved from her, she was suddenly aware once more of her surroundings, and of the hot sunlight beating on her head.

"Well, Cassandra, if you're really not interested in me then you're a damn good actor."

Passion was replaced by anger. "That wasn't fair and you know it."

"I wanted to test you. To see if you spoke the truth. And I don't think you do. I think you're as attracted to me as I am to you. Admit it."

Her mouth was dry, her stomach nauseous. She'd been brought up to be honest, to tell the truth, to live life with integrity. And she did want him—badly.

"I can't."

"Not used to telling the truth?"

Anger flared once more. "Stop! Stop it Dallas. I'm here to do a job. This is not personal."

"You're my Personal Assistant. That's very personal in my book. I need to know what you feel, what you want."

"No you don't, Dallas. *No, you don't!*" She couldn't stand this any more. He was determined to break her down, to find out what was going on. "Look—I just need to be alone for a few moments. Why don't you go inside for lunch and I'll join you shortly."

"You know something? I don't think I've ever been dismissed before. It's a novel experience."

"Please." She met his gaze steadily, desperate that he shouldn't see the cracks that were threatening to shatter her self-possession.

"Okay. But don't be long. We're not finished with this subject yet."

She watched him walk inside to be greeted by half-a-dozen people all intent on pandering to his ego and needs.

I'm frustrating him, she thought, as she walked to the edge of the pool, because I'm not doing the same as the others and he doesn't have my measure yet. She realized that he wouldn't rest until he did. She was like some irritating puzzle he'd worry until he'd solved.

She took a deep breath. She'd never anticipated Dallas Mackenzie would threaten her at this level. This interest in her was unexpected. And even more unforeseen was her response. She'd only prepared herself professionally, but personally he was leaving her wide open.

Drawn by the sound of splashing she took a seat where she could watch the children. They were completely alone.

Anger flashed through her. How could their parents leave them alone in a pool, leave them open to such danger? Irritated she glanced around. There was no-one else about.

A table was set outside for the children.

"Hey kids—why not have some lunch. It's all laid out for you."

"Not hungry," shouted one of the older kids.

Cassandra could understand. Danny used to swim in her father's pool. He could stay in for hours. She blinked back the tears.

She did a quick head count and suddenly leaped up, heart pounding. The boy with the float, where was he?

She dropped her glass, dimly hearing it shatter on the stone pavers and ran to the side of the pool, hand shading her eyes from the glare that reflected off the water. The ball. She could see it bobbing in the middle of the pool. And she could see the boy—upside down, small feet splashing silently from the upturned float which was holding his head securely under water. There was no-one near him, no-one aware of the silent disaster.

"Get help!" She screamed at the kids, as she kicked off her shoes and dived into the pool. She gasped as the cold water smacked against her hot body, drew in a rasping lungful of air and swam over to the boy, grabbed him and righted his now still body.

Above the sound of her own blood pulsing through her head she was dimly aware of the screams and calls of people coming closer. She reached the edge of the pool, choking, gasping with fear and swallowed water. Eager hands pulled the boy from her grip.

She tried to haul herself up but suddenly strong arms swept under her and pulled her onto the side of the pool.

"The boy," she gasped. "Is he okay?" She couldn't see him for all the people who now surrounded him. But she could hear the boy retch and vomit up the water that had threatened his tiny body, immediately followed by his shrill and terrified screams as he came round. Shouts of relief followed and the boy was carried into the house.

"He'll be fine." Dallas slung a large towel around her. "I think it'll take longer for his parents to recover than him."

"Thank God."

"Thank God you were here watching them. Christ knows what the parents were thinking of, leaving the children alone."

"They didn't think." Cassandra's voice was hoarse from emotion.

"They should have damn well thought. If you have kids, you have responsibilities to those kids. Come on—come inside and get changed."

She could barely walk. Her whole body was numb, exhausted, aching. She stumbled and would have fallen if Dallas hadn't been there, supporting her. He picked her up easily in his arms and entered a small guest bedroom. It was dark and cool inside and Dallas gently lay her on the bed.

"Are you okay?"

She nodded, unable to speak, fighting off the feelings of grief and tears that threatened her, hoping above hope that Dallas would go, would stop speaking, would leave her to recover.

Instead he stood watching over her, angry and anxious at the same time. "What were the parents thinking of, leaving their son alone like that? He could have died."

"He didn't though. He didn't die. It's all okay." Cassandra drew her arms around herself, fighting back the tears, trying to hold back the memories.

He sat down on the bed and pulled strands of her sopping hair off her face. A sob escaped her lips and she tried to wrench herself away from him so he wouldn't see.

"Cassandra, are you all right?"

She couldn't answer. She couldn't let herself respond as she had no idea what would emerge. She tried to throw off his arm, struggled to crawl across the bed to the other side, needing to be alone, needing him not to see the grief she kept inside.

But his grip simply grew tighter as he lay down beside her, pulling her to him trying to quell her struggle and calm her. She had no escape. Trapped by his arms, her face away from him, unable to move, she tried to stop her body trembling. She tried to focus on the heat that radiated out from his body, warming her own.

"Are you hurt?"

She tried to speak, but was afraid that the sobs that were threatening would burst through.

He pushed the wet hair back off her face, still holding her close.

Cassandra tried a last attempt to pull away. But he wouldn't let her. Frustration and grief emerged in a wail that escaped her lips before she could stop it. Heaving sobs wracked her body as she struggled to get away and as he fought to hold her. She needed to escape him, escape the room, escape the whole lot of them. The stronger she tried to wrestle her arms away from his, the tighter his hold grew. And still the sobs kept coming. He was not going to let her go until she'd finished sobbing up the pent up emotion, not knowing that it was for guilt: the guilt of letting her own child die, that she cried.

She collapsed against his chest, sobs wracking her body. She couldn't stop shaking but he held her firm. All thoughts of where she was, who she was with, had gone. She could only see the face of her son. The emptiness and pain hit her like a wall. She'd pushed it out, held it back with control, with purpose, but the small boy's near drowning had blown the defenses to pieces. The tears that had been suppressed for so long came in floods. But still he held her.

Slowly she came around. He held her loosely now, stroking her hair, soothing her. She could feel his wet shirt beneath her cheek. She could feel his strength seeping into her, comforting her, upholding her. She wanted to stay that way forever: in a place of comfort from her pain. She knew when she moved, it would all have to start again. What an irony. The man giving her the greatest comfort from her grief was the man who'd caused it. She knew bitterness would follow, but she had no strength for it now.

She had been dimly aware that Lucia had entered and swiftly exited, leaving fresh clothes. She could hear the murmur of people from next door, but inside this place of refuge there was only this man with his arms around her, and the ticking of a clock, steadily marking time.

Slowly Dallas relaxed his hold and drew away from her. She could see the dark stain that her tears had made on his shirt and wondered at his compassion for her. It wasn't what she'd expected from him. Nothing was.

"That wasn't just about the boy, was it?"

She didn't reply, but closed her eyes and pulled away from him, turning to the window through which she could see the rows of orderly grape vines cradled by the rolling hills on either side.

His hand reached out and rested gently on her shoulder. "Lucia left you some clothes. Get changed and we'll go home."

Home. Cassandra closed her eyes again in an attempt to control the conflicting emotions. He rubbed her neck and shoulders. Despite her body's response to his touch she remained looking out of the window, holding herself still, waiting for him to stop.

But he didn't.

"Your hair." He pulled one long strand away from her head. "It's drying into curls."

She clamped her hand onto his, stilling his caress. "I straighten it."

"Why? The straight hair is glorious, but the curly, well, it's very…"

"I know what it is." She turned wearily to face him. "It's an unruly mess. I like to keep things tidy, under control." She looked at him defiantly, daring him to object, as she pulled her hair tightly and twisted it into a merciless knot.

"Let it go, Cassandra. Sometimes things just slip out of control. And I, for one, like it."

"I don't make a habit of letting things go." She tilted her chin as she tried to face him down, dragging up the remnants of her strength from deep within.

"I know that. But I think perhaps you should."

She could have coped if he'd met her challenge with irritation but his quiet words of understanding hit their mark and she was powerless against him, vulnerable once more.

There was a knock at the door.

"Enter." Dallas didn't turn to the door. His eyes were locked on Cassandra's.

"Cassandra! How can we ever thank you?" Lucia looked from one to the other of them and then grabbed Cassandra's hand and steered her to the pile of clothes.

"Dallas! Out you go. I'll make sure Cassandra's okay. We'll be with you in half-an-hour."

Fortified by a hot shower and a strong brandy, Cassandra met briefly with the boy's parents before Lucia showed her a private way to the waiting helicopter. Within moments they were in the air and heading away from Onihau.

It had only been a couple of hours but it had changed her. She could feel it. A barrier had fallen, allowing the grief to slip through and dominate everything. Even her need for revenge, her hate for this man, paled beside it. It had left her exhausted and vulnerable.

He took her hand in his and held it gently. She felt a stirring inside that had nothing to do with her son or the newly cherished boy in Onihau and everything to do with this man beside her.

He drew her hand to his lips. "Thank you."

She looked at him, surprised. "You have nothing to thank me for."

"We have everything to thank you for. I don't know where you came from and I don't know exactly what you want or what you're hiding, but today you saved a family's hopes and dreams."

---

With Rosa away for the week-end, the house was quiet and drowsy in the late afternoon sun.

After making sure Cassandra was comfortable on the settee, Dallas flung open the French windows and walked onto the deck overlooking the scented garden. Bees buzzed heavily from bloom to bloom and cicadas clicked fitfully as a few early ones basked in the hot sun. He looked up at the sky. Clouds were massing and he could feel the prickle of moisture in the air. A storm was brewing.

That brief glimpse at what lay at the heart of Cassandra was tantalizing and he couldn't leave it at that. He wanted to discover more of the mystery behind her grief. For grieving she was. Something had devastated her at her core and he was determined to find out what it was. He had to, because he wanted her and he wanted her to trust him. He needed to break down the barrier she had erected in defense and, to do that, he needed to understand her, to get to know her.

He turned back into the house.

"I'll fix you a drink. What would you like?"

"Nothing. I'm really fine."

"I'll get you a brandy. You're as white as a sheet."

Before he left the room he turned briefly to see her drag her hand half-heartedly through her tangled curls and yawn. She yawned again and lay back on the sun-soaked settee. The barriers were falling. He just had to wait.

She was fast asleep. She looked so fragile: her face relaxed, her slim body curled into the cushions of the chintz-covered chair, all tension drained, lips softened. His hand gripped the brandy he'd poured for her. He placed it quietly on the table, took his own soda water and sat in the chair opposite her and watched.

She awoke suddenly, her disorientation evident in her eyes.

Dallas folded the paper he'd been holding but not reading, passed her a drink and sat back again in the seat opposite her.

"How long have I been asleep?"

"Long enough to get some color back into your cheeks."

"And you've been working in your office?"

"No. I've been here."

He could see that she realized he'd been watching her

while she slept and he could also see that the thought both excited and appalled her. The contradiction was evident in her heated eyes and shifting body language.

"Feeling better?"

She nodded. "Much."

He took pity on her discomfort. "Good—because you've got dinner to cook."

Her laughter turned to coughing as she nearly choked on her brandy. "Very considerate of you, Dallas. I should have realized you had a vested interest in me resting."

Her low laugh unfurled a coil of emotion in Dallas's stomach; it toyed with his feelings in a way that nothing else could. It was the sound of herself, her vulnerabilities, feelings open, guard down.

"I'm not known for my consideration. I believe Rosa has left everything ready, so it shouldn't be too onerous."

"No problem." She rose. "I used to love cooking."

"Used to?"

She paused, nodded and headed to the kitchen.

Dallas couldn't take his eyes off Cassandra's behind in the borrowed jeans. They were faded in all the right places and slightly loose, making her look more fragile. They made a man think of sliding a hand inside and...

He sighed. If only he could drink. It'd been some time since he'd longed for a whiskey, or for a woman, quite so much.

Cassandra placed the empty brandy glass on the table beside the remains of their meal, sat back amid the heap of cushions and sighed. She felt vaguely surprised at how relaxed she felt. With her body curled up in delicious comfort on the soft sofa, she felt almost weightless.

Despite her languor she was very aware of Dallas sitting opposite her, entertaining her with anecdotes with the obvious intention of distracting her from the pain of her memories. And he'd succeeded. All her senses were attuned to him: his physical presence and force of personality and, not least, his sexuality.

As he walked away to refill his glass she allowed her eyes to drift close once more. Suddenly she was aware of the resonant sound of silence. It wasn't menacing as it had been in recent months, when she'd done anything to avoid it, filled as it was with images of pain and grief. Now, it was solid, reassuring—and strangely expectant. She snapped her eyes open.

"You're nearly asleep again." He was leaning towards her, close and observant.

"No. I just feel"—she stretched—"good."

"Come on. You should go to bed."

He pulled her to her feet and her eyes rested on the small creases at the corners of his mouth that formed when he was trying not to smile. She might be the most relaxed she'd been for many months, but she was also the most aroused.

"You should try *not* to smile more often."

"And I should do that because?" He was close now, looking down into her face.

"Because of these." With both thumbs she traced the lines around the mouth, feeling the slight roughness of stubble, aware of the instant change in his manner as he responded to her touch.

He groaned and her thoughts scattered as his lips pressed against hers that parted in immediate response. Desire slid, like liquid silver, through her body, making her aware of every movement of her lips, body and hands. It was as if she were moving in slow motion, with a heightened awareness of every texture her fingers moved over: from the soft material of his shirt, to the hairs on his arms and the tension in the muscles of his back as her hand slid under his shirt.

The sensations intensified as his mouth moved hungrily over hers, until she felt and absorbed every touch, every smell, every taste, as if time had stood still and every nerve ending in her body was attuned to the man whose mouth and body she was exploring with her own. There was nothing else except their bodies—touching, consuming each other—and the sensations that flooded her mind.

Suddenly he pulled away and she leaned in to him, a whimper simmering in her throat, triggered by her need to have him back where he belonged. But he wasn't a man to command, he was a man to entice. Slowly she tilted her head back, exposing her neck, inviting his caress of her body.

Her breath seemed to hold forever until his teeth lightly nipped her neck and she inhaled sharply in a gasp, that turned into a moan as his tongue trailed a scorching path down her throat. There, he kissed her pounding pulse and his fingers swept down her neck, falling to the curves of her rounded breasts just visible above her top.

Then she caught his gaze and the fire in his eyes lit a corresponding fire within her and time suddenly sped up.

He lifted her and her legs embraced his hips while his tongue took control of her mouth. With each thrust of his tongue, she wriggled against him, her hands lost in his hair, her mouth under his, her body a slave to his.

"Cassandra." His voice was husky with arousal. He let her legs fall to the ground, gently holding her until she'd found her feet, swaying unsteadily. "We should go upstairs."

She shook her head; she wanted him now.

His eyes mesmerized her. The cool gray had gone, fired up to the darkened molten steel of a storm cloud. Light glanced off the planes of his face from the wall sconces and darkness dwelt in their shadows. In this unlit corner his face appeared enigmatic, mysterious. She could see and feel only the man he was inside—the real man, not the public figure. And she wanted the real man, more than anything.

She dipped her head and pressed her lips to his chest, her fingers shakily undoing the buttons of his shirt. She wanted to explore his body—its beauty, its strength, its passion. For one night she wanted to consume this man and to forget about the past. She opened his shirt and stood back to admire his tanned and muscular body.

She trailed her tongue down over his chest and stomach, relishing the numbing hairs against her tongue, the smell of his skin. She kissed him and felt his muscles contract under her lips.

Suddenly he pulled her to her feet and stepped away from her decisively, gripping her shoulders with a welcome pressure and control.

"Stop," he growled. "I want to make love to you properly."

He scooped her up in his arms and kissed her, but softly this time, his hand shifting under her as he slammed open the door with his foot and strode across the hall to the stairs.

Within minutes they were inside Dallas's master suite, closing the door with their bodies. He carried her to the bed where she lay, suddenly feeling vulnerable. His eyes swept her body and she was once more struck by how his face was barely recognizable in the soft light.

She was suddenly aware of the silence which surrounded them. It was like the sudden quiet when everything comes together—a solution found to a puzzle, a home found after much traveling. It felt so right.

She reached out to him and he took her hand in his own and squeezed it. And in that brief, gentle grip she knew him once more—his spirit, his body. She didn't want, or need, to know anything more.

She smiled as she reached out for him. She wanted nothing between them now.


Later, much later, Cassandra lay gathered in Dallas's possessive embrace. She felt completely sated, for the first time in her life. She rubbed her cheek against his neck. He smelt like heaven. She breathed him in deeply, wanting to hold the essence of this man for as long as possible. She wriggled closer into his embrace—his arms holding her tightly—feeling secure and at peace. She wanted to remain there forever.

Only the soft patter of rain entering the open window, and the steady ebb and flow of the sea on the shore below, broke the silence. It was like the sound of eternity.

The last thing she remembered was his hand gently bringing her head to rest on his chest and his lips touching her hair, before sleep drifted over her as gentle as his kiss.

# CHAPTER EIGHT

S he was awoken by the cool light of dawn.
*What had she done?*

She reached out tentatively across the bed. Empty—thank goodness. She eased herself out of bed, holding her head as it hammered with the exertion. *Too much brandy.* She groaned. But it wasn't brandy that wasn't making her feel bad. It was guilt and betrayal.

How could she have slept with Dallas Mackenzie after all her meticulous planning? After all he had done to her family?

She sat on the edge of the bed, her head in her hands, pain streaking through her body, her nerve endings aflame with the anguish of knowing that she'd let her son down.

She could have screamed with anger and frustration. She'd lowered her guard because of the emotions of the day before and he'd taken advantage of her vulnerable state and seduced her. No, she corrected herself. She had seduced him.

For once, she'd lived in the moment, with no thought of the past or the future, only the present and she'd taken what she'd wanted, what she'd known Dallas had also wanted. But now she had time to think. And to relive the feelings that she'd spent so many years repressing.

The boy's near drowning had penetrated her defenses, bypassing any thought or pretense. And she'd acted, like she should have acted six months ago, and saved him. She shouldn't have let Danny go with her father on the boat. She'd felt a shadow of doubt at the time, knowing her father to be depressed, but had ignored it. She'd been a solo mum, she'd had work to do, she'd had commitments to meet. And she'd favored them over her own child. She would never forgive herself and she would never forgive Dallas Mackenzie for tipping her father into a suicide that ultimately led to the death of her son. He was culpable and she was going to make him pay.

How could she? How could she have slept with the man responsible for her son's death?

She heard movements—the sound of Dallas coming up the stairs—and shakily she pulled a robe around her. Her heart thumped as he backed into the room wearing only jeans and carrying a large breakfast tray.

"Just toast and coffee—I'm no chef."

The sight nearly undid her. This powerful man bringing her something as homely as coffee and toast. But she held onto the pain and focused on the feelings of hate that had sustained her over the last six months and the revenge that was all she had left. She needed them now.

He turned and stopped abruptly. "Cassandra?" He put down the tray and strode over to her. "Something's wrong. What is it?"

"I've got to go."

"Go? Where? In case you hadn't noticed, the boss is requiring you to be at the office this morning."

"That's it. That's just it. You're the boss. This isn't right."

"It looks very right to me."

"But—"

His mouth cut her words short. She lapsed into forgetfulness, for one long moment, aware only of the needs of her body, and his, before reality hit her once more.

"It looks very right to me," he repeated hoarsely.

He brushed his lips against hers and then against her momentarily closed eyes. She could feel him inhale, almost drink her in. It had to stop. She snapped her eyes open and pushed her hands flat against his chest. His hands closed more tightly around her arms in response.

"Let me go. I have to leave. Rosa and the others, they'll be here shortly."

"So?"

His eyes narrowed. A flutter of panic ran through Cassandra's gut.

"So, I don't want them to think that I've..."

"You've slept with me? Why not? What's it to do with them? This is between us, Cassandra. You and me. No one else." His eyes narrowed. "Or is there someone else?"

She shook her head. She could hardly tell him of the ghosts who were also involved. "Please, let me go."

"Not yet. Not until you tell me what this is all about. Why the ice queen melted so spectacularly yesterday and why the woman who was so willingly mine, so lusciously without inhibition, has come over all virtuous again. What's going on?"

"Yesterday—last night, it wasn't the real me. I don't know, it—"

"It *was* the real you. I know. I was there. It's this, this coldness, I don't understand. I knew you were hiding something the moment I met you. My few enquiries came up with nothing. I could have looked further into your background, but I decided not to."

Relief swept through Cassandra.

"No," Dallas continued. "I prefer to do this the hard way. It may be more time consuming but, somehow, I think it will be more interesting."

"There are some things you have no right to know, that are nothing to do with you. It's none of your business."

"You've *made* it my business." His low tone was barely more than a growl. "You made it my business the day you walked into my office demanding an interview, demanding my attention. Well you have it now, whether you want it or not."

He took one quick step towards her and stood close, so close her cheek rasped briefly against the stubble of his chin as she instinctively turned to face him. She had no choice but to close her eyes against his black gaze as his lips found hers and his body pinned her against the wall.

As he pressed against her, she received his kiss more deeply, her body responding, burning with lust. She wriggled against him and he groaned and dropped her hands. He pulled her to him tightly, their bodies hard against each other's.

Afterwards she couldn't remember who'd made the first move—who it had been who'd unzipped his jeans. Whether he'd lifted her, or she'd jumped up into his arms, her legs curling around his waist, she couldn't have said. And it hardly mattered, for the effect was the same.

There had been no rational thought, only pure, unadulterated lust as they'd come together, except this time without protection.

But the thoughts had slowly returned and, along with them had come the guilt... and the apologies.

"I'm sorry," he'd said."I was rough and I wasn't prepared. I should have used protection."

She'd shaken her head. It had been the last thing on her mind.

He'd tied the robe around her body and held her briefly, before releasing her. "Go and get dressed."

And she'd gone. Glad that she could allow the tears to flow freely out of his sight. There had been no pointing in staying, no point in saying anything because the truth of her feelings wasn't acceptable to either of them.

She'd fallen in love with him. And she could hardly believe that, despite this, she was still going to ruin him.

*What had he done?*

He turned away as she closed the door quietly behind her.

*What had he done?*

He'd let it happen—the thing that he'd always made sure to avoid. He'd seen, in the depths of those blue eyes, her soul and it had touched him. It should never have happened.

He couldn't deny this, it was too powerful. The lovemaking had been on a different scale to anything else he'd ever experienced. Her body was responsive to his every touch and her skin smooth as silk and exquisitely sensitive. But it was more than that. He connected with her at a level which he couldn't begin to describe.

That she'd had a change of mood in the morning wasn't surprising. He knew she had secrets and somehow they involved him.

He turned on the shower, bracing his body against the icy spray.

He knew one thing for sure. He hadn't spent his whole life avoiding relationships, to cave in now. No. She obviously regretted it and so did he. The way he'd taken her that last time—roughly, without finesse—proved that he was exactly like his father deep down, violent and selfish. It must never happen again; he must avoid getting close to her, must keep it purely business. The feelings might be there but they could not be acknowledged, because he knew that it would hurt her in the long run. Just like his father had hurt his mother. He pulled on a clean shirt and jeans and pushed his hands through his hair. This was wasting time. He had work to do.

---

It might be a Sunday, Cassandra thought briefly looking at the pile of papers on her desk, but Dallas obviously didn't imagine she needed a break. Which was fine with her because it meant she'd be alone. Alone with security clearance and time to further her plans. The admin work could wait.

As she carefully negotiated her way through the company databases, digging deeper into its confidential areas, she found it more and more difficult to concentrate. She shook her head. Ridiculous. After months of preparation she was so close to keying in the commands that would rob Dallas of his wealth—would ruin him and his family—and all she could see were his granite eyes, heated by lust, looking into hers, holding her as they climaxed; all she could feel was the slope of his back, narrowing to his buttocks and the muscles in his arms and chest, powerful and sensual. She flushed with the thoughts that flooded and warmed her.

*Concentrate, Cassandra.*

It didn't take long to get to the point she'd been anticipating for so many months. But instead of proceeding, she stopped. She jumped up and looked out the window searching for the usual sense of peace which the view brought her. But neither the rippling emerald hills nor the bay brought her peace today.

All week, she'd expected to see evidence of Dallas's ruthless business acumen, expected to see trails of where his thoughtless lust for money had driven him, expected to see the wreckage of lives, or hopes, all buried under an unstoppable force of money-making.

She'd found none of it.

Perhaps she'd simply been working on the wrong files? Perhaps he'd covered his tracks too well? But she knew that, without a PA and busy as he was, no tracks had been covered. All the correspondence around his business dealings over the past year had been laid bare for her inspection. There had been nothing untoward.

It wasn't the Dallas that she'd expected, nor the one the popular press enjoyed to feature so much.

Was his one error of judgment the sly take-over of her family's company that had destroyed them financially and emotionally forever? Was this the one time that he'd acted irresponsibly, hastily, not checking the background papers, not seeing how emotionally unstable her father was, how vulnerable they all were? Not being able to see the devastating, far-reaching consequences of a single decision on her family? Was that the only time?

One error had been enough, though. It might have been out of character but, for whatever reason, Dallas Mackenzie was responsible for the deaths of those she loved most. It only needed to have happened once.

She withdrew a memory stick from her pocket and sat back down at the desk. She'd spent enough time at college with her computer geek friend to know it could be done and a few recent meetings with him had been sufficient to nail down the details. She broke through the final security barrier with ease.

It didn't take her long to get to the point of no return. Her fingers hovered over the keyboard. One key stroke and she could destroy his wealth. He wouldn't know where to look, where to find it. It would simply have vanished into the ether.

But phrases from his correspondence, decisions he'd made, memories of his interactions with people, flitted through her mind. Instinct told her he couldn't do such an act; her time with him reinforced that instinct. She hesitated, holding her throbbing head in one hand while she circled the keyboard restlessly with the other.

Suddenly she pushed her chair back from the desk. She couldn't do it. She couldn't believe he would have made the decision to ruin her father. He must have been coerced. He mustn't have been in possession of all the facts. Something didn't fit. Something wasn't right.

She had to leave. If her instinct was right and he wasn't responsible for the death of her father, then she would be wronging an innocent man. She would be guilty of a crime that he would never forgive and for which she could never forgive herself.

If her instinct was wrong, then she didn't want to know. Because she couldn't live with the fact that she loved the man responsible for the death of her loved ones.

The light of the computer pressed into her darkness.

She closed her eyes briefly before rapidly entering a series of commands to exit the program.

"Sorry, Dad; sorry, Danny—I can't do it."

Her whisper sank into the rhythmic sound of the sea as it crept up the shingle beach and crawled lazily down again.

She clicked the laptop closed.

She knew it spelled an end, not just to her plans for revenge, but to the very thing that had kept her going. She had nothing else. She acknowledged her love for Dallas as if appreciating a beautiful object she could never possibly own. She couldn't let it affect her, couldn't let it near her. She had to leave.

She took one last look around the elegant room that was her office, complete with the now familiar heirlooms of the Mackenzie family, and closed the door firmly behind her.

She was dressed and ready before first light. She waited until the first lonely calls of birdsong penetrated the pre-dawn light before taking one last look around the room and quietly opening the door. She held her shoes in one hand and her bag over her shoulder as she avoided the creaking boards and tiptoed down the stairs.

So far so good.

There was no sign or sound of activity in the kitchen and she knew that Rosa slept in the other wing. She just had to unlock the door. She'd seen Rosa lock up at night so knew the drill. As she eased the lock across, there was a sound like a dull thud that caused Cassandra to pause. Surely that came from outside? She hesitated, her ears straining to hear the slightest sound.

Nothing. She must have imagined it.

. . .

Dallas waited until the soft thud of the automatic garage door clunked into place before entering the garden. Immediately his gaze was drawn to Cassandra's window.

No lights. It was still early. She'd be asleep.

The thought of Cassandra in bed did nothing to calm him. Visions of their lovemaking had haunted his mind and body throughout the day and night. Despite the company of beautiful women at dinner and afterwards, he'd seen only her eyes in their faces, felt nothing but the want of her in their every look and gesture. He was besotted and he wasn't happy.

He slung his jacket over his shoulder, despite the chill of the early morning. He hesitated as he crossed the courtyard and looked up at her open window, the gauzy curtain flipping in and out with the breeze. A vision of her lying on the bed, asleep, naked under the covers, filled his mind: hair, curling in damp tendrils close to her head, the rest fanned out over the pillow.

He shook his head. That way lay madness.

Then he heard the front door click and a shadow emerge, hesitantly, onto the verandah. He withdrew behind a high trellis and watched. If it was a burglar leaving, then he was just in the mood to meet him. A surge of adrenalin swept through his veins. He tensed, ready to attack.

Once the heavy door closed, the intruder stepped out into the garden and then stopped suddenly. Dallas shrunk further back. He could grapple with the burglar now. But something made him hesitate as he watched the outline that grew more distinct as it came closer. He knew who it was, even before the faint waft of her scent reached him.

She was leaving.

But he would follow.

Cassandra couldn't help herself. She closed her eyes and breathed in deeply of the garden's heady fragrance that hung on the cool morning air. It tugged at her heart. She felt a connection, a belonging, here at Cliff House she'd never felt anywhere else. With anyone else, she corrected herself.

She had to go. There was no other way.

She shivered and continued her slow walk through the tangle of shoulder-high wild and cultivated flowers, their aromas pungent in the early hours before the sun had risen. Drops of dew fell on her face from the flowers and newly spun spiders' webs that trembled, as if in anticipation of the day ahead. The very air seemed to hover, suspended in the early morning hush. She caught her breath and felt her skin tingle. It was a magical place.

She looked suddenly behind her. Despite the still languor of the garden, she felt on edge, thrilled—almost as though she weren't alone.

She shrugged off the feeling. Stupid. If it was too early for Rosa it would definitely be too early for any of the other staff, or Dallas who preferred late nights to early mornings.

The thought of Dallas made her move again. Pushing the top-heavy flowers to one side, shedding petals as she went, she made her way to the wooden door in the garden wall which led to the bush path and on, down to the road. From there she would be free of the estate and free of Dallas Mackenzie.

Once she shut the door behind her, she was immediately enclosed in a different world. Native bush rose above her, darkening and dampening the air. She took a deep breath of the earthy, pungent air, and followed the path, its twisting way indicated by a trail of solar-powered lamps. Without them she would have been lost in the dense bush within moments of leaving the path.

Strange sounds made her jerk her head up and peer into the bush canopy, into the thin strip of lightening sky visible directly overhead the path. But it was only huge silver ferns that coiled and shook over her head, only the ancient vines that creaked in the wind.

The place was raw, untouched, wild. Her heartbeat quickened as she tried to contain a shudder, not of repugnance, but of fear. It seemed to challenge her, speak to her soul.

"No," she said, her voice hardly audible to her ears. "It's too hard. I can't go there." She couldn't risk letting go of her defenses—not yet, if ever.

She turned suddenly. What was that? A noise. She backed towards one of the lights and felt a soft brush against her cheek like a lover's kiss.

Longing ground down into the pit of her stomach. She turned to find moths—huge, beautiful in their moonlight colors, silver, gray and luminescent green—flitting together in the glare and warmth of the light, drawn together in an instinctive, life-long quest to find their mates.

One fluttered once more against her hair and she drew away from the light, mesmerized by its beauty and persistence. She edged back one more step and then turned, drawn irresistibly to face the path once more.

"Cassandra." His voice was low, barely heard but felt with a force that made her stagger back.

"Dallas!" She could feel the blood drain from her face as a wave of sick shock swept her body at seeing him before her, unheard, undetected.

"Expecting someone else?"

"No, I..." Her voice faded away. Talking was impossible through her suddenly dry throat and Dallas's appearance had driven all thought from her head.

"Couldn't sleep?"

She shook her head.

"A walk before work, then?"

She swallowed and gulped in the cool air. "I don't usually go for pre-dawn bush walks with my luggage." She flicked him a rueful, uncomfortable smile.

"You're leaving then."

She was struck by his tone: low, resigned, disappointed somehow.

She nodded. "I have a taxi coming."

"Can I ask why?"

"I think you know why."

"And you'd leave without a word?"

"There's nothing to say. I've done some good work for you. Left my resignation on the desk. I hardly thought you'd object, you couldn't even bear to see me yesterday." She couldn't prevent a bitter tone creeping into her voice.

He turned his head quickly to one side, his mouth a hard line, his hands pushed into his pockets as if for control. "Come on. I've been busy. And you would hardly have welcomed by presence."

"It had to be professional. Not personal," she added in a lower tone.

"You showed me that it's all personal. That everything we do touches someone."

She jerked her head up to his, seeing him standing closer to her. "I have to go. I can't take this now."

He took a step closer still. "You must listen. I don't want you to go. I—"

"Yes?"

She paused waiting for him to continue. But there was no response. She stepped away.

"I need you."

She stopped dead in her tracks and turned to him. He hadn't moved. He still stood, filling the narrow streak of light with his dark presence. She could sense he was holding back. She knew his instinct would have been to act, to follow her with the intention of physically making sure she returned with him. But he controlled that instinct. He didn't move. He was giving her the choice.

His restraint melted her intentions like a soft kiss on a worried brow. She dropped her bag. "What did you say?"

He stepped towards her then, into the light, and she could see the winged creases around his mouth crinkle as he tried not to smile. "You're not going to make this easy for me are you Cassandra? I said, I need you."

"You need me?"

"I need you." His smile vanished as quickly as it had arrived and he glanced down briefly at the path before raising his eyes to hers once more. "I need you to be my PA. It won't get personal again, I promise. I won't let that happen. I need you with me, because—we work well together. Besides I haven't time to recruit another PA, it'll take too long."

She knew him. Knew his self-delusion, knew his inability to face his emotions. She also knew that she loved this man and couldn't leave until she discovered the truth about the events that led to the deaths of her son and father. She had to stay, to find out exactly how Dallas was implicated in the tragedy that had blown her family to pieces. If Dallas meant what he said, he'd keep his distance. He'd give her the time she needed to discover the truth.

"On a professional basis only?"

"Professional only. You have my word."

He extended his hand and gripped hers. The power of his touch sent trails of heat blazing through her hand and body.

"It's a deal," she said huskily, hoping that they weren't making a deal that neither of them could keep.


The bush lightened innocently around them as they returned to the house. Gone was the brooding elemental gloom that reduced life to the essentials. The soft light tamed it, made it manageable once more.

Rational thought returned and Dallas was relieved. He had no time for all this emotional stuff. Personal or business, it was all the same to him. The thought of her leaving was just, well, untenable. Having her by his side was right. And that was all there was to it.

He adjusted his step to Cassandra's. She was walking slowly: tired, he assumed. He held back a stray fern for her, briefly glimpsing the delicate lines of her nose and cheekbones, highlighted by the blush of early morning sun.

He simply needed her. He couldn't explain it any better. Searching for words was like groping in the dark, in an unknown place, for something he'd never seen before. There was little point when he knew what he wanted. Her. And he knew what he had to do to keep her—engage her brain rather than her body.

He closed the gate, leaving the cool bush behind them and the garden, flooded with rosy light, spread before them.

They walked like strangers side by side up the brick path towards the house whose windows shone in the early morning light.

"I'm giving you responsibility for new business. I'll get

Jen to cover the routine PA work. The first presentation is this morning. There's some proposals to work on and then there's some work coming up with Bill Northam. He's an old family friend. It's good, solid business. I thought you'd appreciate that for a change."

"Sounds good to me. What time is the first presentation?"

"Ten. You'd better use the next few hours before breakfast to prepare."

"I'll be ready."

He caught his breath at the sight of her hair curling like a halo of light around her face and then looked ahead firmly.

"Make sure you are."

## CHAPTER NINE

The house was still quiet. Cassandra had come to love the early morning starts. Alone in her office she had time to collect her thoughts and find some peace.

She'd agreed to stay over two months ago and she'd not regretted her decision. He'd kept his distance, believing that was the only reason she stayed. But he was wrong. She'd stayed because she loved him and wanted to discover the secrets surrounding the acquisition of her family's business. She had yet to find out the truth, but time had just run out. She had to leave. She was pregnant.

She rubbed her forehead.

She had thought she could continue working with him until she was discovered. But the pregnancy test showed otherwise.

She had to go. He had made it clear that he wanted no-one in his life long term, woman or child. She lightly caressed her stomach. But it would be a new chance for her. A sister or brother for Danny. A fresh start. In the mean-time, she had a meeting to attend.

. . .

Dallas jumped into the external elevator just as Cassandra was on her way to the boardroom to meet Bill Northam. Horizontal rain slashed the harbor as she switched her eyes from the view to the elevator buttons.

"Which floor?"

"Same as you."

She smiled at him. "I can manage, thank you Dallas."

He smiled, the same, ironic smile back. "I'm sure you can, Cassandra. But as it happens I'd like to say hello to Bill again. Then I'll leave you two to get down to business."

He held the door open for her and followed her across the plushly carpeted foyer to the boardroom, where an elderly gentleman sat, dapper in a pin-striped suit, complete with a wide-brimmed Akubra hat. A huge grin split across Bill Northam's face at the sight of Dallas.

"Dallas! How are you my boy?"

He welcomed Dallas like a son, engulfing him in a bear hug and slapping his back.

"Very well, Bill. Good to see you out and about again. Got some new business I hear?"

"Can't keep an old dog down." Bill guffawed; his pleasure at seeing Dallas again was obvious.

Cassandra wondered how far back they went.

"Glad to hear it. Bill, meet Cassandra Lee. She's my new PA/Project Manager who will be working with you on the business. I need her to make sure you don't pull the wool over my eyes."

"You certainly wouldn't want to be blind with this beautiful young lady around. How are you my dear?"

Cassandra felt an unaccustomed blush rising.

"Very well thank you, sir. I'm looking forward to working with you. I've done a little research and think I can see where we can add value to your present portfolio."

Bill winked at Dallas. "Brains and beauty. Only the best eh, Dallas?"

Dallas smiled back at his old friend, without looking at Cassandra.

"I'll meet you and Cassandra upstairs in the apartment later and we'll have dinner. It'll be easier for you than braving the weather. It looks like a storm's brewing."

"Very thoughtful of you, Dallas. Mind you, a storm is never far away in Wellington." He sat back down and gave Dallas an exaggerated salute. Give my regards to your mother. Still on the Mainland?"

"Still in Glencoe, yes. She prefers the seclusion."

For the first time, the big grin on Bill's face drooped. "Yes," he said thoughtfully. "Probably wants some peace and quiet after what she's been through, if you don't mind me saying."

Cassandra felt Dallas's gaze drop to her briefly before returning to Bill.

"Old friends, Bill. You can speak your mind with me."

"Only way to do it, my boy. My memory's too bad for prevaricating. I can never remember what my story is. So best to keep it simple. You go on. I think I'm in very capable hands with Cassandra. Off you go, son."

---

After three hours with Bill, discussing different projects and strategies, Cassandra didn't believe Bill suffered any decline, mental or otherwise. Or if he did, she wouldn't want to have done business with him before. He was as sharp as they came and she'd learned a lot.

"Shall we call it a day, sir?"

"Bill. Please call me Bill. Yes, I think we ought. I'm not

as young as I was. So tell me, are you enjoying working with Dallas Mackenzie?"

Cassandra busied herself with collecting the various investment statements and documents together. "Of course. The portfolio is varied and interesting."

Bill leaned closer to her. "No my dear. I mean do you enjoy it? He's a good man you know. He's not his father, for all the similarities. Not that he knows that."

Bill paused, his gaze focusing on the mid distance. Cassandra shrugged as she closed down the laptop. Bill's gaze, instantly alert, switched to her.

"Not that you'd know Dallas's father, would you?"

"No. Dallas doesn't talk of him and I believe he's dead."

"Yep. Eight months ago. The drink finally got him." Bill shook his head. "Sad. He was a man with great potential and did great things in his time. But the drink was his failing. Drink, frustration. Married the wrong woman." A shadow of sadness passed across Bill's face until he looked once more into Cassandra's own curious gaze.

"Eight months ago?" It was eight months ago that her life had changed. And the fact that tragedy had befallen Dallas's life at the same time, struck her forcibly.

Bill nodded. "Yes. Nasty business. Dallas and his father never got on, as you probably know. But Dallas always gave him a second chance, and a third chance. They all came to nothing. The last chance was when he persuaded Dallas to let him look into a small takeover in Boston he'd got a bee in his bonnet about. Seemed he'd had dealings with the owner some years before." Bill pursed his lips and shrugged. "Dallas was just pleased to have him occupied for a few months. He never imagined that his father would pursue an old feud and destroy this man's life." He shook his head. "Of course, there was no going back once his father had done the deed. Dallas had to sort it out with James's help. The company was rotten through and through and all Dallas could do was sell it off in parts in the hope of salvaging some of the investment. Dallas's father died in his sleep shortly afterwards. A stroke, I believe."

Cassandra froze. Aghast, she listened to the inevitable.

"Apparently the owner shot himself. Nasty business. It seems he'd been trying to cover up the rotten accounts for some time. But, out of respect to the remaining family, Dallas insisted it be hushed up."

"Dallas's father's mistake," echoed Cassandra, the words formed stiffly on her lips.

"That's right. Not that Dallas looked at it that way. He blamed himself for the whole mess, furious at himself for letting his father make such a blunder. He couldn't have known though. No one could. Frank deceived everybody, every day of his life. And he made his poor wife's and sons' lives hell."

Bill gazed out across the stormy harbor, shaking his head. Cassandra was thankful his entire focus was on the Mackenzie family and their misfortunes and he was totally unaware of the effect his news was having on her.

She pushed her chair away from the table and rose, pushing herself up unsteadily. She moved deliberately and picked up some coffee cups and deposited them on the trolley at the far end of the room. She stood there, clutching the cold steel handles of the trolley and seeing only Danny's face, feeling only Danny's need. She rubbed her hands together in an effort to stem the physical pain that pushed through every vein, every nerve ending in her body. She looked up at the ceiling in an effort to contain the flow of tears and took a deep breath before turning back to Bill.

She returned to the table aware that, despite the pain,

she felt intense relief. Dallas was innocent. He was guilty only of giving his father one last chance. The man who she should have been targeting had died shortly afterwards. She took a deep breath and focused on the papers in front of her.

Bill suddenly turned. "While ago now though. And I just hope that Dallas has put it behind him. He's got you now to help him, hasn't he?" He peered short-sightedly at her. "Are you well my dear? You're the color of chalk."

Cassandra plumbed the depths of her control and retrieved a bright smile. "Hungry, that's all. Let's go and meet Dallas."


Cassandra felt as though a light had been lit in her heart. Sadness still dwelled there but not the heavy, suffocating, maddening fear that accompanied it. That was there no more, lifted with Bill's words.

With each step she made towards Dallas's penthouse, half-listening to Bill's conversation, offering an arm when his stiff limbs needed some assistance, Cassandra rejoiced.

Flashbacks filled her mind: of Dallas as they'd first met: cool, inscrutable—the ubiquitous strong man.

Of Dallas, affectionate and concerned at the pool.

Of Dallas, making love to her, driving her into an ecstasy that was all-consuming.

She allowed herself for the first time to think of the man untainted by doubt, of the integrity and kindness that lay beneath the hard exterior. She allowed her love for him to flood her body with its heat and intensity without restraint and to command her heart unchecked. All her instincts had been proved correct. While she'd always known, deep down, that he was innocent, she'd never permitted herself to surrender completely to her feelings. Now she could.

But it had no long-term future. She knew that. He wanted no long-term commitments, particularly with someone who'd betrayed his trust.

But she wanted one more night: a night of passion before she left forever. Could she persuade Dallas to mix business with pleasure? He'd kept his distance for so long, she didn't know what he thought or felt about her. But she was determined to find out.

The doors slid open and they entered the foyer of the apartment. The maid immediately opened the doors and ushered them inside to where Dallas was waiting, hands thrust into his pockets, eyeing the fury that was unleashing before them across Wellington. He turned to welcome Bill.

"How did the meeting go?"

"Superb, Dallas. Extremely well. I feel thoroughly spoiled with all the attention. Just what an old man needs."

"Don't give me that 'old man' nonsense, Bill. You're as sharp as a tack, haven't changed in all the time I've known you."

"And that's some time, eh lad?"

Dallas smiled, his affection for Bill obvious.

"A lot of water under the bridge. Anyway, your Cassandra—"

"Not *my* Cassandra, Bill."

"Oh, don't give me that modern crap. Let an old man say it as he sees it. Your Cassandra is going to take you far, Dallas. She's just what you've been needing for years. Brains and beauty—she'll be indispensable before you know it."

"I appreciate the compliments, Bill," said Cassandra.

"But how about you two stop talking about me as though I'm not here?"

Dallas looked at her with a cool, inscrutable expression. "I fear you're right, Bill. She will be an asset to our company. Indispensable though? Nobody's indispensable."

She accepted a drink from the maid and sat on the leather sofa, trying to hide the sting she felt at his words. She knew by now that truth was important to him and that he always meant what he said. It was as if he were giving her a warning not to expect too much.

"Come now, Dallas. That's not true. The journey's better if you've got company."

"How is Dorrie?"

"Same." Bill's face collapsed into sadness. "Rarely recognizes me. But she's being well cared for."

"I'm sorry."

Bill shrugged. "Anyway, I hear she has a regular visitor —a tall, dark handsome man who brings her gifts?"

Dallas grunted. "She's a lovely lady. She was always very kind to me."

"She loves you, Dallas."

Cassandra looked up at the softness that was in Bill's voice to see a brief wordless connection pass between them, before Dallas turned back to the picture window. Over his shoulder she could see trees straining in the face of the oncoming southerly and the Inter-island ferry slowly edge its way into dock, no doubt relieved to be out of the six meter swells of the Cook Strait.

"The storm seems to be settling in for a few days. Hope you're not expecting to fly out tonight, Bill?"

"No. Always keep my options open when I'm in Wellington. Got a couple of meetings lined up and some pleasure. Tomorrow night I have tickets to the opera. I'd be delighted if you could both join me."

Dallas looked briefly across to Cassandra. "I'm out of town on business tomorrow, but I'll be back in time to come. Cassandra may have other plans."

She knew he was giving the chance to opt out. He was keeping his word about separating business from pleasure. And she appreciated it. Dallas always kept his word. It was part of the reason she loved him.

"I'd love to come, Bill."

Dallas shot her another quick glance before indicating they should sit to eat.

"I didn't know you liked opera." Dallas's tone was quiet. He could obviously sense something had shifted. She'd enjoy watching him work it out.

"So many thing you don't know about me, Dallas."

Bill looked from one to the other, a smile playing on his lips. "And won't it be fun finding out, eh Dallas?"

Dallas raised an eyebrow. "Apparently."

---

A quiet day in the office was exactly what Cassandra had needed. She had to have time to come to terms with the truth around the deaths of her father and Danny.

There was the fact that the family company had been in worse shape than she'd known. Her father had kept things close. No-one had known or suspected how bad things had got. And then there was the fact of Dallas's non-involvement.

For the past six months she'd studied both the man and his work to make sure that she could destroy him. All the pain had been channeled into accomplishing this end. And now, after her initial joy at discovering the man she loved was guilty only of loyalty to an errant father, she was left with feelings of frustration and emptiness. They were the only things that were holding back the flood of pain and loss that she'd never accepted, never considered, never had time to deal with.

She had the rest of her life to live without her precious son and her beloved father. How could she do it? Her hands automatically went to her stomach where her and Dallas's child was growing. She would have to do it, for the baby's sake.

She stared out into the far distance, rippling hills now misted with rain clouds and felt her eyes burn as they slid down to the cityscape beneath her window, trying to focus on the small square windows of offices in the buildings opposite. They showed small glimpses of life, as office workers moved around, lived their lives concerned with paying for their children's education, coaching their children's soccer, nursing their sick children. It was something that she would never have with Danny.

"Ready to go, miss?" She hadn't heard the knock and jumped up when she heard Todd's voice. He was taking her back to Cliff House to get ready for the opera.

She nodded.

"Everything all right?" He approached her, frowning.

She turned quickly back to the window and with one hand scooped up some files and with the other wiped away the tell-tale tears that had run unnoticed down her cheek.

"Sure. Let's get going."

Cassandra opened the sash window and closed her eyes against the cool damp air.

She began to unbutton her shirt but her fingers fumbled. All her movements and thoughts, seemed slow, studied, difficult, as though simple actions required great effort, as though she were wading through water.

A sense of numb confusion pervaded her. It was as if her mind had stalled, stopped thinking and feeling at any depth as a self-protection mechanism. The truth was she'd never anticipated beyond this point. She had never contemplated a future beyond ruining Dallas Mackenzie. Now she was beyond the point of imagining. Now, there were no plans, no strategies to shore up her innermost feelings of pain and guilt. She knew she would not be able to keep the pain at bay for long. She would have to face the feelings she'd buried eight months earlier on the day she'd given up hope of ever seeing her son alive again.

But not yet. She would have tonight first. She would inch her way to feeling, moment by moment and savor the sensations the night with Dallas would bring her—whatever they might be—that she'd blocked from her life all those months ago.

And then tomorrow she would be gone.

Tomorrow she'd have to face the pain and guilt of her loss and the knowledge she'd very nearly ruined an innocent man. The man she loved. The man who, she knew, would hate her once he'd discovered the depths of her lies and intrigue. She knew he'd hate her because she hated herself.

But she'd have one night before he hated her: a night in which he would make love to her.

· · ·

As she was leaving her room she caught sight of herself in the mirror and stopped abruptly. She didn't recognize herself: curly hair licked her shoulders and tumbled down her bare back, framing a face dominated by her dark red lips and eyes that shone with a message that was purely sexual.

And then there was the dress. The demure trappings under which she'd denied her sexuality had been banished. In their place was a dress she'd bought to wear as a slip underneath a sheer dress. But, on its own, it was perfect for what she wanted.

Seduction.

Light shimmered over the sheer red satin, highlighting every curve and hollow of her body, leaving little to the imagination. Just one look at her and Dallas would know what it was she wanted: him—fully and completely—but only for tonight.

The front door slammed shut on a gust of wind followed by voices at the foot of the stairs. Dallas had arrived home. She glanced at her wristwatch. They'd be leaving in an hour. She had time to complete everything.

She packed slowly. She didn't have much but, as she folded her business clothes, she relived the moments she'd worn them, the moments she'd been close to Dallas, had felt his touch on her sleeve or had noticed his eyes drop to her dress.

The thoughts intensified the slow burn that smoldered inside.

An hour later she was ready. Her bag packed, the room empty, a spare bedroom once more. Ready for the next PA. The thought caused her pain; a tiny stab of jealousy, deep within, found its mark. She ignored it. She had no right to be jealous. She had no rights at all, not after what she'd tried to do to Dallas.

She took one last look out the window at the brooding island around which the sea swirled, confused by the twisting direction of the wind and the turn of the currents.

Some things never changed. She could never imagine Dallas away from here. He was too much a part of it, of its history and its future. But she, like the swirling tides, the flotsam and jetsam taken up by the waves and flung far afield, was moving on.

She leaned her forehead against the cool pane of glass and closed her eyes, trying to calm the heat that was building within. The wind moaned and the waves crashed on the shore far below. Now they were joined by other noises. Dallas had re-entered the hall, talking on his cell phone.

It was time.

She placed her packed bag by the door where Rosa would find it when the taxi came, picked up her wrap and purse, and closed the door quietly behind her.

She paused on the unlit landing and looked down the sweep of stairs into the large hallway. Dallas was leaning against the wall, with his back to her, one hand clamping a cell phone to his ear, the other pushing back his hair. The dinner jacket hung from his broad shoulders as only a bespoke tailored jacket could. She moved forward to see him more clearly, making no noise but still she could see a sudden tension appear in his shoulders. He turned slowly around and returned her gaze, not speaking and not revealing anything but their connection.

She could hear a voice on the other end of the phone as

he dropped it from his ear and turned it off, without taking his eyes off her.

"Cassandra?"

His voice was barely a whisper: a question asking more than confirmation of her identity. And she knew her real answer would be conveyed, not by a word, but by the emotions she could no longer keep from her voice.

"Yes." A statement of readiness.

He went to the foot of the stairs and waited.

As she walked down the long sweep of stairs, her stilettos clicking on the wooden risers, his eyes left hers for the first time and swept the length of her body. She felt as if she were walking down the steps naked and, from his expression, she knew that that was just what he was seeing.

As she stepped off the bottom step, Dallas took her hand.

"You look amazing."

"I feel amazing. But that's nothing to do with the dress."

"There's nothing much of the dress."

Cassandra laughed, breaking the tension, filled with happiness at the sight of Dallas's rare flash of smile. "I wish you would smile more often."

He brought her hand to his lips, contemplated it as if deep in thought, before turning it and kissing her palm. "I feel like smiling when you're around."

He wasn't smiling any longer though, and nor was she, as they moved closer, absorbing each other's presence, inhaling their scents.

Suddenly, the kitchen door slammed and Rosa emerged.

"Todd has the car ready Dallas. You ready? Ah, Cassandra. Don't you look pretty? Where you going Dallas? You're on time for once, don't disappear."

"I have something I want to show Cassandra." Cassandra smiled as Dallas retreated backwards towards the study. "It won't take long."

Rosa banged the kitchen door shut once more, muttering as she went.

As the door closed behind Rosa, Dallas extended his hand to Cassandra. She took it immediately and he gripped it tight and pulled her into the study and closed the door.

"What's this all about?" His thumb moved heavily in her palm, stirring her already acute sensations even further.

"It's about this moment, Dallas. Nothing else."

They stood close, connected only by their hands, his eyes roaming her face. His nostrils flared as they inhaled her scent and she could sense his growing excitement only in the tensing of his jaw. He contained it all.

"Why the change of heart? Did Bill put you up to this?"

He was close but not close enough. He still had no idea why she was really there—thank goodness—and no idea of what Bill had said to enlighten her.

"Of course not. No, this is just between you and me."

"You know I want you, Cassandra. I've wanted you from the moment we met. But you're my employee and I don't intend to break your contract. You're too valuable to me. Does that mean you're willing to be my lover and my PA?"

She drew closer, her lips not quite touching, luxuriating in the feel of his quickened breath upon her cheek. "Definitely." She breathed the words onto his lips and then pulled away, relishing the lust in his eyes, the throb of the pulse in his neck. His lips, however, were compressed and firm. He was determined to be in control.

But it would be her that would be in control tonight.

"I want to be close to you tonight, Dallas. That's all that's important."

She drew away from him and, following her lead, he opened the door for her to pass through into the hall.

"Tonight it is then."

# CHAPTER TEN

Dallas tried to inhale Cassandra as she passed a hair's breadth away from him. Her scent, a heady mixture of perfume and her own unique fragrance, intoxicated him. He could never get enough. The sight of her breasts, unconfined by a bra, shifting as she walked, made him want to grab her there and then, and make passionate love to her. But something held him back.

He feasted on her rear view, on the way the fabric's nap lightened where it grazed her rounded behind. Again there was no visible sign of underwear to impede his imagination. His hands itched to pleasure that body that was made for love-making.

But more than that he wanted to pleasure her mind, her spirit and that meant that he had to wait, he had to follow her cue. Cassandra had taken control and he was more than happy to wait and see what she had in mind. Somehow, he was sure it would be worth it.

. . .

Outside the trees that surrounded the house on the upper side of the cliff, strained against the fierce wind. A shiver ran through Cassandra's body and she pulled her wrap around her shoulders. She wasn't cold. Here, in the walled garden, the flowers merely trembled as the wind raged overhead. It was anticipation of spending the night with Dallas that aroused and stimulated her senses.

She looked up at him as he pulled the door closed, his eyes fixed on her. She wondered how she could ever have been intimidated by this man. He had his weaknesses—a temper, alcohol—but he'd mastered them, and his passion, his loyalty, his kindness and his integrity shone through. She trusted him with her life.

"What are you thinking?" He touched her cheek.

"I'm thinking you trick people, Dallas."

His eyes narrowed. "You know I don't."

"You fool them into thinking you're a tough son-of-bitch. But you'd do anything for anybody—except yourself."

"Don't overdo the analysis Cassandra. I know who I am and I know what I want. And just at this moment I want you. That has to be enough. Is it?"

"Just this moment is fine. It's all I want, too." Cassandra moved closer to him, drawn into his space, impelled by a primitive instinct she could barely control.

His lips curved slightly as he approached her and bent his head to hers. Instinct made her lift her lips to his, but he paused and simply looked at her, the expression in his eyes more tender than she'd seen them before. She closed her eyes and parted her lips as his hand brushed down her back and rested briefly on her bottom. The hovering sense of anticipation solidified into a electric flash of fire inside her as he kissed her softly on the lips. Her breath caught in her throat as he pulled away once more.

"Shall we?" It was only the low, roughened tone which betrayed his need.

She opened her eyes to see him watching her, his eyes dark, his mouth firm once more. "Shall we, what?" All thought, all sense of purpose had fled her mind.

"Go?" A smile twitched at the corners of his mouth as he took her arm and indicated they should move through the garden.

"Of course." She took a deep breath. She would have only one night with him and she was determined to enjoy every minute of it. She could wait for the satisfaction only his body could bring her and she knew that Dallas would make the waiting almost as pleasurable as the consummation.

The scented garden had never looked more beautiful, more abundant, more full of promise. A flurry of wind showered them with droplets as they passed under the rose arbor. Cassandra felt with remote fascination a trickle of cold rainwater descend her back. She shook the droplets off her hair, made wild by the damp, wind-tossed air.

Once outside the garden wall, the fury of the storm was fully evident. The bush creaked and groaned with the erratic pounding of the wind gusts that whined over the roof iron of the outbuildings. The sea roared at the foot of the cliff. She paused for one moment and closed her eyes, acutely aware of her heart beating in accord with the raging elements. Then she felt Dallas's large hand enfold over hers and pull her out of the chill air and into the car.

"You're crazy tonight, Cassandra."

She turned to meet his look. She was surprised. She'd never seen such an unguarded expression of warmth on his face. She'd always known it was there, deep inside, but so hidden, even from himself.

"I feel as I've been freed. But I'm not crazy—well, only about you." She moved closer to him, watching as a flicker of emotion cross his face. "And only for tonight." She added, knowing his fear.

Her face was close to his and she parted her lips in invitation. He sat back and thrust the keys into the ignition.

"Later. Be patient." He turned to her, a light smile playing on his lips. "God knows what I did to deserve you." He shook his head. "But I thank him for the day you walked into my life."

Trembling with unfulfilled need, Cassandra smoothed her dress and sat back. God knew and so did she. And, at some point, so would Dallas. And when he did, he would never want to see her again. The thought was sobering. It was all she needed to recover from the lust that had threatened to overtake her.

"You okay, Cassandra?"

She summoned up a smile. "More than okay. But, you're right. Perhaps I am just a little crazy tonight."

The car thrummed into life under them as he turned the keys. "I love crazy." He began the slow drive down the twisting road. "But we have to go to the opera. We promised Bill. But I want you more than a little crazy when we come back home. And I'll make sure of that. I'll have you so hot that you'll by putty in my hands."

"First mistake, Dallas. I rather think you'll be the one who won't be able to wait." Her hand languidly trailed down his thigh. She smiled to herself as the muscles in his leg tightened in response to her touch.

"We'll see about that." He accelerated sharply onto the highway.

. . .

Dallas tried to concentrate on the weather conditions, work, anything to take his mind off the trail of heat that Cassandra's fingers had left. Just as well she'd taken her hand away. Any longer and he'd have had to pull over.

"Talk to me." His voice was a low growl.

"Anything in particular?"

"Anything at all. Anything to keep my mind off how I want to take you back to the house and take that dress off you. Try telling me why you changed your mind. Why you decided to make yourself my exceptionally personal, Personal Assistant."

"It's a woman's prerogative, to change her mind."

He risked a glance at her under a passing street lamp. She wasn't as light-hearted as her response suggested.

"Come on. We've only worked together for a couple or months but, in that time, I know you don't act on whims. You're considered, responsible, ethical. What's changed?"

Silence greeted his comment. He could sense a shift of mood as they overtook a stream of cars on the two-lined highway, before emerging from the hills into Wellington city, its open harbor spread before them.

"Ethical?" Her voice was barely audible above the hum of the car.

"Of course. It's a part of you. Everything you've done in the business has been based on integrity and honesty. I can assure you I've noticed. Honesty is a rare commodity in my family. My father anyway."

"Tell me about him."

"He was a liar, a drunkard and a bully."

"And that's why you don't drink alcohol?"

"Of course. I'm too much like him." He couldn't help the bitterness creeping in. "And without the alcohol I reckon I'm less likely to be a liar or a violent bully."

"Dallas, listen to me. With or without alcohol, I cannot, for one minute, imagine you lying, cheating, bullying, whatever. It's just not in you."

He snorted. "You don't know me, Cassandra. You think you do, but you don't. Stay clear. If you're still interested in tonight, in the now, then I'm your man. But there is no long-term future for me with you, or for me with anyone." He paused before revving the car to pass a lorry. "I can't risk it."

Her hand cupped the back of his head in a fleeting caress that was achingly loving. Instinctively he tilted his head back to allow it to rest in her hand, but she was gone. She edged her body towards him.

"You're so afraid." The words were hushed, in tones so slight and gentle that they reached into his heart, striking at the core of who he was. He could only shake his head abruptly. He couldn't trust himself to speak immediately.

"You don't know me," he repeated. "Don't presume to think you do." His fist banged the steering wheel in frustration and anger. He regretted the outburst as soon as it had erupted. A glance confirmed that Cassandra had turned aside and was focused on the traffic they were speeding past.

"You see." He could feel his voice tight with control now. "It's never far away. My temper is there, waiting and I don't trust it. And nor should you."

"I'd trust you with my life."

He met her quick glance, her eyes as calm and serious as her voice.

He shook his head. "Don't go there. I can't do it."

"Just because you don't have faith in yourself, doesn't mean that others can't have faith in you." She twisted in her seat to face him. "Look Dallas, I've been with you day after day, and some nights too, for months now and I've seen you in every situation. You may have been angry, but you've always controlled it. And even if you did give vent to it, I trust you. You wouldn't harm me, or anyone else." She turned to face the oncoming road. "It's other people you shouldn't trust, not yourself."

Unwanted emotions of longing, confusion and, yes, fear, swamped Dallas as he drove, foot flat against the floor, skimming through the stormy night down into the Wellington harbor basin. He barely registered the spray of the sea as it pounded the motorway, drumming against the roof of the car. The rhythm of the windscreen wipers, slapping away the fierce rain, barely intruded on his thoughts. Only the movements of the woman beside him penetrated his brain: the woman who knew how to move him physically and emotionally and challenge his own deep-rooted notions about himself. She, alone, occupied his mind.

The wet tires screeched as they pulled up in the undercover car park.

Dallas hadn't yet spoken and Cassandra deliberately didn't break the silence.

He needed time to come to terms with the fact that he was driven by fear—until then he would never be free to be himself. But she couldn't help him make that journey. She wanted to tell him how much she loved him but she knew that her love was of no interest to him.

She shivered and pulled her wrap more tightly around her body as Dallas opened the car door. Silence fell around them, deep as the hurt she knew she'd inflicted.

She stepped out the car and reached up to touch his lapel, her hand flat against his heart. She wanted to reach out, show him that he wasn't alone, that there was someone who cared very much about the real Dallas Mackenzie.

"I meant it, Dallas. You're not your father."

He gripped her hand tightly in his own. "I am as I am. And there's nothing to be done about it."

"That's enough for me."

He dragged her hand away and kissed it, pulling her closer to him with his movement. "Good. That's all I want too—you, tonight."

He embraced her lightly, running his hand down her back, mussing her hair with his lips. She closed her eyes as sadness overwhelmed her. She knew one night would never be enough.

"That's what you want too, right?"

She nodded, not trusting herself to speak, simply relishing the feel of his hand, pulling her towards the exit with a purpose that echoed the strength of her own needs.

A wall of warm air and noise hit them as they entered the foyer of the theatre and made their way to the ticket office. She'd always loved opera, even as a young child she'd been moved by its larger than life sounds and sights.

While Dallas talked with the box office clerk, Cassandra looked around. The modern theatre was spacious and light with fine acoustics. People greeted each other loudly and sipped from elegant champagne flutes. Cassandra recognized some establishment figures—politicians and leading businessmen—and yet other trendier groups who led the Wellington art scene and made it the cultural capital of New Zealand.

At the feel of his touch on her back, she turned to see him frowning.

"Looks like we have the box to ourselves tonight. Bill's taken ill and isn't coming."

"He seemed fine yesterday. I hope he's okay. Should we go to see him?"

"He doesn't want us to. He's left a message with the clerk. Just a sniffle, he said. It's not like him though."

Cassandra couldn't tell whether Dallas was pleased or not to be alone with her. "It's okay. I don't bite." She smiled at his quizzical look. "Not in public anyway," she couldn't help adding, trying to lighten the mood.

She was rewarded with a curve of his lips and a spark of humor in his eyes.

"I wish I could say the same about myself. Come on, let's have a drink."

As they walked through the crowded foyer, Cassandra wondered if it was possible for Dallas to enter a public building without being greeted every two seconds. Wellington was a small city and Dallas appeared to know everyone in it. Anyone who mattered, that was.

But Dallas steered clear of joining any of the groups. Politeness didn't enter his vocabulary and Cassandra had to smile, pleased for once at his arrogance. He was a man who knew what he wanted and didn't waste time on things that didn't matter. And it seemed that, for now, she mattered to him. And, looking at his tall figure—dark, commanding, distant to everyone else but her—she knew that she was where she wanted to be. He had a past he couldn't rid himself of, just as she did. She just hoped hers wouldn't catch up with her before the night ended.

"Dallas! Cassandra!" Guy and Lucia, his friends from Onihau, greeted him warmly.

"Dallas! You've been keeping a low profile of late. What

have you been up to?" Lucia kissed them both on the cheeks.

"Just business, as usual."

"Is that right, Cassandra?" Lucia asked, disbelieving, turning her away from Dallas and Guy for a more private tête-à-tête. "If it's been just business, then business seems to really agree with you." She took a step back, surveyed Cassandra's appearance and laughed appreciatively. "What's work to some is pleasure to others, I guess. Anyway, good to see you looking so well."

"Never better. Look. I'm sorry about my over-reaction at your party."

"No. It was my fault entirely. I should have kept my eye on the little critters myself. But not having any ourselves— not yet anyway—I just didn't think. But you did though, didn't you?"

Cassandra nodded and took another sip of wine, hoping she'd change the subject. Lucia's thoughtful expression made her uneasy.

"Do you have children?"

Cassandra's heart sank. But there would be no more deceit. She nodded. "Once I did."

Lucia's hand came around her shoulders. "Aah, I see. It all makes sense now. Does Dallas know?"

Cassandra shook her head and smiled a little, trying to reassure Lucia.

"Okay. I won't say anything."

They turned back to the men.

"Dallas, I hear James is returning to New Zealand. Is that correct? Can he really have had enough of New York?"

A cold shiver ran down Cassandra's spine. She'd met James briefly in Boston after he'd been sent by Dallas to sort out a few things with the company. It had been an accidental meeting and she'd refused to stay. But he'd remember her if he saw her again. She just hoped that when he heard her name he didn't make any links with one Sandie Carstairs, formerly of Boston.

"He'll be here for a while setting up a new business in the South Island. How long he'll stay is anyone's guess."

"When will he be arriving?" Cassandra's voice seemed softer than the others, betraying her nerves.

"In a few months."

Good. She'd be gone by then. The thought sent a confusing blend of relief and sadness through her.

"Well," Lucia said, raising a teasing eyebrow at Dallas, "it'll be good to see him again. He'll bring an element of sophistication back to the Mackenzie clan." She smiled. "Don't look at me like that, Dallas. You know you're not in his league when it comes to smooth-talking and charm." The smile turned into a laugh and she turned to Cassandra. "Is he, Cassandra?"

Cassandra looked up at him and held his gaze. She wasn't laughing. "No. No smooth talk. No charm..."

Heat flashed through her body as his eyes seemed to devour her. She didn't know how long their gazes had been locked until Lucia touched them both on their shoulders and inclined her head to theirs. "You two should get a room."

The bell sounded to indicate the performance was about to start and Lucia and Guy disappeared to their seats.

"A room, Cassandra?"

She tilted her head to one side, basking in the blatant innuendo of his few words. He wanted her and just needed the signal. He'd have to wait.

"The box, Dallas." She grinned as the look in his eyes

only intensified behind the control he put in place. She'd enjoy watching him lose that control. Later.

The news that James was returning—albeit after she'd left— had cast a shadow over her. And Dallas had registered the change. She was aware of his concerned glances. He could obviously sense that something had happened, that something had taken the edge off her excitement.

She sat back and closed her eyes, ostensibly to better listen to the music. In reality, to come to terms with the realization that her time was short. She couldn't be here when James arrived. She had no doubt that he'd recognize her, even if her name meant nothing to him.

The music changed. A woman's strong contralto soared out into the theatre, filling every corner with emotion. She snapped her eyes open. Dallas was no longer sitting facing the stage. He'd shifted his seat so that he sat facing her. His gaze was stern, frown lines furrowed between his eyes that were dark and unreadable. But she could read his body language all right. He was angry.

"What is it, Dallas? What's the matter?"

"I'll find out, Cassandra. I'll find out what you're hiding from me."

"There's nothing—"

"Don't bullshit me, woman." The cold anger in his voice shocked her. "I know you. Like I've never known anyone before in my life. I feel you." He was furious—furious and frustrated because his feelings had overtaken his control. He screwed his hand into a fist and banged it onto her armrest. He leaned over her, his voice dropping to a whisper. "I feel you, Cassie. You must know it."

The singer's voice rose as if it came from inside

Cassandra and she felt her strength and power flow through her. She pulled up Dallas's fiercely clenched fist to her face and pressed her lips up hard to it.

His head dropped down, away from her face and she could feel his anger dissipate.

"Dallas?" She knew what she wanted and she wasn't prepared to wait any longer.

He looked her directly in the eyes. "Are you going to tell me what's going on?"

"I'm going to show you. It's all about now, remember?"

He stood up, turned his hand within hers and grasped it firmly, pulled her to standing.

Wordlessly, without facing her again he pulled her out of the box and along the corridor towards the exit.

## CHAPTER ELEVEN

They ran through the rain-lashed streets of a deserted Wellington. With no coat, it was only moments before Cassandra was soaked through. But she felt nothing but heat—heat that came from within and from without, flowing from Dallas, his hand still tightly in control of her own.

Breathless, she glanced at him. He appeared oblivious to the rain that ran in rivulets down his face and back. His dark hair was streaked darker by the rain and the shadows of the night were reflected in the stark planes of his face.

Within minutes they were at the Mackenzie Building and for the first time since they were in the theatre, Dallas turned to Cassandra. But not to speak.

He cupped her face and kissed her with a passion heightened by the run through the streets. Their combined need had roared from the slow simmer, that had been repressed for so many months, to become a raging fire that gathered momentum with each passing minute and could only be expressed through each other. Their bodies were pressed tight against each other, their mouths and hands and legs shifting, moving, enveloping each other. Both needed to consume and be consumed.

Finally they parted. Dallas released her and stood back, breathless. Cassandra could see the force of effort it took for him to focus. He looked around, as if dazed and patted his pockets.

"Where's my damn security card?"

She slipped her hand across his chest and plucked it from his inside pocket and grinned. "Here—"

He cut her short with another stormy kiss before swiping his card.

The private entrance bypassed the security guard and cameras, and they stumbled into the softly lit lobby, Dallas carrying Cassandra. They continued to kiss as they reached the elevator. He backed into the wall but couldn't reach the elevator button. She stretched out her leg, and kicked the button with her foot.

His lips left hers for a moment. "Thank you."

Her breathing came hot and hard. "My pleasure."

The elevator doors opened and they entered.

Slowly he let her slide off him. He pushed away the wet hair which clung to her face and shook his head as if in disbelief.

"You were right. You *are* crazy tonight," he breathed, as his eyes devoured her.

She put her hands around his neck and pulled him closer. "But... are you?" she asked, with a teasing kiss.

"Only about you," he said.

For the remainder of the ride up to his penthouse neither spoke. They simply drank in each other as if they could never get enough.

Intermittent shadows flickered over his face as the elevator moved onto the exterior of the building and the lights of the office tower opposite alternated with the darkness of the passing floors.

Finally, they emerged above the neighboring buildings into the night sky with the dark pool of the harbor spread beneath them, dotted with late ferries and boats returning to harbor for the night.

The elevator stopped and the door opened. Cassandra stepped out, her heels clicking on the hard marble, just as they had done a lifetime—or so it seemed—ago.

She felt his hands around her shoulders as he kissed her neck. "You're beautiful." He whispered huskily into her ear.

"Because you make me feel beautiful."

"No, because you are. Would you like a second opinion? The security guard would probably be happy to oblige. Ow!"

Cassandra withdrew her teeth from his fingers. "Perhaps that's how you really lost your finger. In a fight, yes, but with a woman."

"You're asking for it Cassie."

"I certainly am."

He withdrew, eyed her cagily and opened the door for her to enter.

She entered the apartment, flicked on the lights and dimmed their glare. She might be about to seduce the man she loved, but she wasn't going to do it under the brilliance of a ceiling full of twinkling white halogens.

She turned and smiled, enjoying the blatant lust in his eyes and wanting to prolong it. "Drink?"

"Are you toying with me woman?" She heard him slam the door close behind her.

She could feel his eyes on her as she strode over to the fridge and peered inside. The cold air hit her in a wave that sent a shiver over her skin. "Whatever gives you that idea?

Just thought you might be thirsty. What would you like, soda water, tonic, mineral water?"

"I'd like you to keep looking."

"So you could—keep on looking?"

"Yep. But I'm not just looking, I'm imagining too."

"Really? Imagining what? Some late-night business to accomplish."

Cassandra stood up and opened a bottle of soda water. Its content ballooned up and escaped over the top, fizzing over her hands. She licked her fingers free of the stickiness, before looking up at him.

He hadn't moved.

"No business. Nothing like that. I'm imagining taking off your clothes and making love to you, as I've been wanting to do for months."

"And how, exactly, will you do that?"

"I'm afraid, my darling, that finesse won't be at the top of my list, not at first anyway."

She cocked her head to one side and took a sip of the soda water. "So there will be more than once?"

"That," he said, reaching out for her, "you can guarantee." He set aside the soda water and thrust his fingers through hers and gripped her hand. "I'll have you again. And then again. Because this is only the beginning."

Cassandra struggled to control her arousal. "I told you that you'd be desperate for me by the end of the evening."

She let him lead her into the bedroom, but there she decided to turn the tables. She gripped the lapels of his jacket and pulled it off his shoulders until his hands were captured in its folds.

"You're at my mercy now."

And, it seemed, as she pushed him back onto the bed, he had no problem with that.

Wellington harbor was lit by a soft gray light, calm and peaceful, as if the storm had never happened. Cassandra lay awake, watching the hills on the far side of the harbor slowly change color. She'd miss it. Wellington. And him. But she couldn't stay. He'd hate her when he found out, either through James or his IT team.

She turned to Dallas, sleeping peacefully beside her, one hand possessively resting on her hip. He had an almost serene look on his face. But how long before the serenity evaporated, leaving hatred in its place?

Carefully, she slipped her body away from his hand. He moved slightly but didn't awaken. Quietly, she walked away from the bed, away from him, desolation filling her soul at the thought of him hating her. She would be gone before she had to witness his disillusionment.

The shower was hot and cauterizing. It sealed her feelings and it sealed her fate. Dressed, now, in the coldly crumpled dress, she stepped back into the bedroom.

He was propped up on his elbows as if he'd just woken up. "You're leaving?"

"I have to."

"Why? Where are you going? It's Sunday. Your boss surely doesn't make you work on a Sunday."

She smiled, despite herself. "Strangely, it's nothing to do with my work."

"Really? Then you must have a life. Your boss didn't want to hire someone with a life."

"I know. I got him to hire me under false pretenses."

"Really? Tell me more." He reached over to try to grab her. She moved back. They stared at each other.

"I can't. You'll find out."

He sat up then, grabbed her hands and held them tightly. "What's this all about Cassandra? Tell me. Enough of your games. Where are you going?"

"Away."

"Where to?"

"Dallas—"

The phone rang. He ignored it, his eyes fixed on her. "Go on."

Cassandra waited, the phone rang and rang. "Aren't you going to answer the phone?"

Angrily Dallas picked it up. "What the hell—"

His words were cut short by what he heard on the other end of the phone. He continued to stare at Cassandra, frustration and anger simmering as he listened. "I'll be right down."

He dressed quickly and roughly smoothed his tousled hair with his fingers.

"I have to go but I want you here when I get back. And then we'll discuss this. No more mysteries. I won't be long. Just some IT mix up."

The door slammed shut and she rose off the bed. It was time to go.


"You see here, sir." Dallas looked over the technician's shoulder and watched the screen. "We were doing a random check and discovered the security had been bypassed and your personal financial accounts accessed."

"How the hell could this have happened?"

"If you watch, we'll see the key strokes that have been recorded." The techie began the sequence and Dallas watched how an unknown assailant had lain siege to his finances.

"And then it stops."

"There? Don't tell me he was just looking."

"Looks like she was either flexing her muscles, showing you what she's capable of—and it was extremely clever—or she had a change of heart."

Dallas went cold. "*She*, you say?"

"Yes, sorry sir, we know the culprit is. For all her skill she didn't attempt to hide her identity."

Dallas didn't ask because, in his heart, he knew.

"Do you want to know her identity, sir?"

"I think I know. It was Cassandra Lee wasn't it?"

The techie nodded, embarrassed. Presumably their relationship had become common knowledge.

How had he allowed himself to get into this position? He'd always prided himself on his invulnerability on all fronts: business, personal, emotional. And here he was duped by this woman and nearly destroyed by her.

"You want me to begin legal proceedings?"

"No. I'll deal with it."

Dallas rose from his chair with effort. Cassandra's betrayal pressed on him like a weight, as if all the crazy feelings of the previous night had solidified into a hard and heavy stone that dragged him down, from the inside out.

But he could also feel the stirrings of anger surging within: an anger he knew would never end.


Even before he entered the apartment he knew what he would find. The room was empty. No message, no note. No trace of Cassandra remained.

He wandered, as if in a dream, into the bedroom and plucked up a pillow and held it to his face, inhaling her scent. He'd wanted her more than he'd ever wanted anything or anyone in his life. But all she'd wanted was his money. Her "mystery" was now crystal clear. She wanted to steal his money and ruin him.

What a damn fool he'd been. He ripped the pillowcase in half and flung it across the room.

There was only one question he wanted to know an answer to. And that was why she hadn't finished the job. Was it fear of being caught? Couldn't have been. Or else she would have covered her tracks better.

A fleeting thought that she didn't proceed because she'd fallen in love with him, occurred to him. But he dismissed it. She'd said she was crazy about him. But she'd said a lot of things hadn't she? Many of them had been proven to be lies. How could he believe anything she had ever said?

He picked up the phone and spoke briefly with Rosa.

So Cassandra had always intended to leave. Her bags had been collected the previous night by taxi and deposited downstairs with security. All she had to do was collect them on her way out this morning.

The scheming woman had everything planned down to the last detail. Including last night. Somehow that seemed a worse betrayal than attempting to ruin him.

He dialed her cell phone.


Watery sunlight filtered through the high windows of the busy railway station. Cassandra could only just hear her phone ring above the public announcements and the shouts of the school children as she waited for the small country train that would take her to a new life.

"Hello?" She could barely hear her own croaky voice.

"Why didn't you finish me off as you intended?"

"I—"

"Come on Cassandra. It's all I want to know. It's all I want from you. Surely you can give me that?"

His freezing tone made her shiver. There was a long pause.

"I made a mistake."

"You made a mistake!"

She pulled the phone from her ear at his raised voice. "Yes, I did. And I'm sorry."

"Why? Just tell me why. What was it all about? Did you really hate me so much? Or did you need the money? I'd have given it to you if you'd asked."

"It wasn't as simple as that."

"The truth is always simple. Try me now."

"It's too late. I deceived you Dallas—from the very start —and I know that you won't ever be able to forgive me."

"How? How do you know that?"

"Because I can't forgive myself for what I've done in the past, and what I nearly did to you."

"I don't understand."

"That's best. I'm not the woman you thought I was."

"No you're not. You're just like all the rest, aren't you, Cassandra? Out for what you can get." She could hear the ice-cold anger and hate emanating from his words.

"It's true." Cassandra tried not to choke on the tears that streamed down her face. "I'm not the fresh, bright woman without a past who can fit into your perfect world. I'm flawed."

"Flawed is fine. Deceit and dishonesty isn't. I won't be seeing you again."

"I understand."

Before she could say goodbye, he cut her off. And he had every right to do so.

She rose from the seat, hands instinctively holding her

stomach and looked around. She had to think of her baby now. She grabbed the bag and pulled it down the platform towards her train. She had just enough money to get clear of Wellington and then she'd make a new life: one in which she could atone for the guilt she felt over Danny's death— she'd never put business ahead of her child again—and one in which she could try to deal with the heartache of loving a man who despised her.

# CHAPTER TWELVE

"I caught up with Guy and Lucia at the weekend."

James sat back on the leather couch, a picture of perfect ease, his smile as warm as his eyes and Dallas remembered how he used to envy James his charm. While life still seemed as easy for James, as it seemed hard for Dallas, Dallas's acceptance of his own fate made it easier to also accept his love for his brothers, James and Callum.

"In the Wairarapa?"

"Yep, one of their intimate gatherings of a couple of hundred people. I thought you'd be there."

Dallas twisted in his seat, rose and clicked on the light, absently looking out across the harbor. "Not in the mood."

"Not since a certain woman left your life?"

Dallas looked sharply at James. "If you're referring to a certain PA who attempted to ruin me, then you'd be right."

"Um." James took a sip of his whiskey, his blue eyes that girls found so irresistible, narrowed as they watched Dallas. "But she didn't, did she?"

Dallas swept up some papers and dumped them into a filing tray, as if unconcerned by the turn of conversation, while inside his heart beat furiously at the conflicting memories of Cassandra. "What?"

"Ruin you."

"No. Could have done easily. Probably realized she'd be found and jailed. I'd not have rested until I found her."

"But you didn't try to track her down when she disappeared?"

"No point. Nothing to say."

"From what Lucia was telling me, I imagined you'd have had plenty to say."

Dallas contented himself with giving James a dirty look. He checked his watch. "Where's Callum?"

"You know him. Won't want to be wasting time on small talk. He'll be working. He'll turn up just before we're due to leave for dinner." It was James's turn to glance at his watch. "About now."

As if on cue, Callum strode into the room—taller than both of them, dressed in casual clothes—and poured himself a drink while nodding in greeting to his brothers.

"Have I interrupted something?"

"I was just telling Dallas he should track down the woman who tried to ruin him."

"And why would he want to do that?"

"Hey, stop talking about me as if I weren't here, will you?" snapped Dallas.

"Because he's fallen for her big time and doesn't understand why she did it," continued James.

"And you *do* understand, I suppose, with your extensive experience with women." Callum laughed.

James grinned a disarming smile. "It's true, I have extensive knowledge of women. However"—he cast a sly glance at Dallas—"in this case it's not required. I happen to have a very good idea what motivated her. Trouble is Dallas doesn't want to hear."

"Dallas *does* want to hear," Dallas said returning to the table and sitting down opposite James once more. Callum continued to prop himself against the wall, keeping half an eye on the expansive view as if ready to bolt outside at any moment. "What do you know?"

"I recognized her straight away. Lucia had taken some snaps at the party you attended with Cassandra. I'd know that face anywhere. Beautiful." James paused and his eyes never left Dallas's. "I briefly met her in Boston after we destroyed her father's company."

Dallas didn't move. His mind raced over James's words, sorting through the facts, the implications, even as his physical body stayed stock still. "Carstairs & Sons?"

"That's right. Except there were no sons by the time it was inherited by Cassandra's father. Only one daughter who had her own high-flying career as a business consultant."

"Tell me everything."

"I don't know everything. Only a few facts, gleaned from my time trying to tidy up the mess that Dad had left with the takeover. She was a widow—her husband had died shortly before leaving her a solo parent."

"She has a child?"

"*Had.* You know the father shot himself on his boat?"

Dallas clamped his hands to his head as a memory slapped him full force. "Christ. The boy who drowned, whose body was never found. It was her son?" He looked up into James's eyes which were full of sympathy now. James nodded.

Dallas swore under his breath and jumped up. "She blamed me. I was the face of the company. You were there as the company's representative but it was me who took responsibility for it. She came all this way to ruin me. To try to—" He shook his head. "Christ!"

"Yep. Cassandra Lee, known in the States by her maiden name of Sandie Carstairs, wanted to devastate you in the only way she thought you'd feel. Your bank balance."

*Danny Lee was Cassandra's son.*

He understood at last. The pattern pieces, so random before, instantly formed a picture—a huge picture—of pain, loss and deceit. He felt at that moment, perhaps one small sliver of the pain that she'd experienced and would continue to experience for the rest of her life.

*His* Cassandra.

And he'd rejected her without finding out why. Why hadn't he trusted his instinct about her, that she was a good and true person? Why hadn't he investigated her background, her motives, more deeply?

Because he'd almost been expecting to be hurt when he'd fallen for her and he'd taken the first excuse that had presented itself to get out of the relationship. He'd slipped back into his old cold ways because he didn't have the courage to make himself vulnerable.

What was she doing now? She obviously had nothing. He had to find her. He jumped up and paced first one way and then another, raking his fingers through his hair. He turned to see James and Callum exchange concerned looks.

"I had no idea." And he'd no idea he could feel such pain.

"For Christ's sake, Dallas. Get on the bloody phone and find her and then go to her and sort this out." Callum's authoritative tone cut through the chaos that raged through Dallas's brain.

"Always the direct method, Callum." James's voice was laconic despite his obvious concern over Dallas's reaction.

Callum drained his glass and placed it squarely on the table. "Anything else is a waste of—"

Dallas didn't wait around to hear the end of the sentence.

## CHAPTER THIRTEEN

He'd known where she was. Not what she was doing, not where she was living, but he'd known the name of the sleepy town in which she'd chosen to hide. Any more knowledge would have been too difficult to deal with—might have tempted him to act on it, like he was doing now.

The slam of his car door echoed around the wide street of the sleepy town and a lone truck roared up the street, a curious sheepdog somehow keeping its balance in the back, eyeing him through the dust as it sped by.

The bookshop wasn't hard to find. He crossed the large grassy square, fringed with century-old plane trees, and stood in the shade of one as he watched Cassandra move around the shop. She was wrapping up a book for a mother and child.

She was so beautiful. Even clad in a simple shapeless dress, she was elegant and poised. Her curls were twisted up in a loose bun and tendrils framed her face. She turned suddenly and looked across to the child and he saw a softness in her expression that he'd not seen before. She smiled up at the mother, a smile full of warmth and compassion, and handed her the book and change. After they'd left the shop, she turned away and gazed into the mid-distance for a minute, her expression pensive.

What are you thinking about Cassandra? About your son? About what you've left behind? He dare not frame the question he really wanted the answer to—whether her thoughts ever strayed to him.

He watched as she stretched out and rubbed the small of her back. As she arched her back, easing some deep-seated ache, her dress tightened around her, revealing a very rounded, pregnant stomach.

He slammed back against the tree as if he'd been struck. Pregnant? How far gone? Was it his? Of course it was. And anyway what did he care whose it was so long as she was with him?

A cold sadness crept through his veins creating a physical ache in his body that he knew he could never relieve. His pig-headedness, his inability to trust his instincts about her had led to her having to experience all the trials and joys of pregnancy alone. No-one to support her as her body adjusted to its new inhabitant, no-one to share the experience of witnessing the baby's heart-beat for the first time. She had been alone, serving behind a counter, when he should have been caring for her. He'd have had the best obstetricians, the best of everything, if only he'd known, if only he'd followed his instincts and tried harder to discover her secrets.

Pregnant though? A cold sweat prickled his brow as he calculated how long ago they'd made love without protection. It must have been six months ago. Six months. His child was growing and nearly ready to enter the world.

But a child? He realized with amazement that his determination never to have children had dissolved, his fears had paled into insignificance when confronted with the stark reality of the existence of his and Cassandra's baby.

He pushed himself away from the tree and felt a curious light energy ignite somewhere deep inside of him and radiate out through his body. As he crossed the road he recognized the feeling as happiness. Was this the Dallas Mackenzie who had vowed never to marry and never to have children? No. He wasn't the same man and he was looking at the woman who made him realize that he had been living in fear.

Even if a friend or relation had been perceptive enough, or brave enough, to tell him he was afraid, he wouldn't have listened. The difference was in his feelings for Cassandra. They forced him to look at himself and acknowledge the truth of her words.

He knew now that he was a stronger man than his father. It's true he would never test himself with alcohol, but he could control his temper and he could look after and cherish a wife and family. But only one wife in particular. He ran the last few steps across the street, each stride strengthening his purpose and determination. He wouldn't let Cassandra and his baby get away from him this time.

He stepped into the small shop, the old-fashioned bell jangling to herald his entrance and, as Cassandra turned to him, her smile froze on her face and she dropped a book.

He closed the door behind him and flicked the "open" sign to "closed". He didn't approach her immediately. He needed to give her time.

"What do you want?" Her voice was a hoarse whisper.

"I'm looking for something."

He stepped towards her and she gasped as he reached down and picked up the book she'd dropped. He handed her the book and walked away abruptly to a wall lined with books. She obviously needed time. And he'd give it to her because he had no intention of leaving here without her.

She cleared her throat. "If it's a book, you've come to the right place. Anything else and I'm afraid you're out of luck."

"Is that so?" She was wrong, because today was his lucky day. He was in the right place at the right time. He turned to the row of brightly colored book spines and ran his finger across them, stopping on a random book. "So what would you recommend? Something like this?" He picked it up without looking at its cover.

She shrugged. It was her only movement. Her face was flushed and her eyes wide, as she stared at him, obviously wondering what the hell he was doing there. Well he didn't intend to tell her straight away. Some things couldn't be rushed.

"Possibly," she said glancing at the cover, "if you're interested in greyhound breeding. Are you?" She looked back into his eyes. He saw the spark of humor there.

He smiled in response. "Not recently. Although you never know." He pushed the book back on the shelf.

She plucked another book from the shelf. "Perhaps something more like this?"

He walked up to her and took the book from her hands and turned its cover to him. "Growing Old-fashioned Roses." He looked up at her and smiled. "That's more like it."

"Do you think you have anything to learn? Your garden is spectacular already."

He inclined his head. "I'm glad you think so. But"—he cocked his head to one side and held her gaze—"there's always something new to learn."

"You said once that you kept the rose garden because it pleased your girlfriends. Admit it, you like flowers."

He shook his head slightly, scarcely aware of what they were saying, only aware of her gradual relaxation, the glint of humor in her eyes, the slight, sweet curve of her lips. "I would never admit that."

"Because?"

"I have a reputation to uphold."

"Perhaps your reputation attracts the wrong sort of girlfriend."

"Perhaps. But I can win them round."

She shifted away. "So confident. Seriously, Dallas, why are you here?"

"I want to talk with you."

"Not shout at me, not call me names, not do any of those things I deserve?"

He shook his head. "Nothing like that. Just talk."

She must have detected in his tone something of the calm certainty he felt because she suddenly nodded, as if convinced. "Okay. Would you like a coffee?"

He smiled, relieved. "Thank you."

She put her hands in the pockets of her dress and pushed them forward, making sure that the dress didn't flatten against her stomach. She was trying to hide it from him. He sat down on one of the brightly colored easy chairs, arranged for the casual browsing of books, and looked around. "Nice place you've found here."

"Yes," she called from out the back. "I was lucky."

He winced at her choice of word. "You deserve some luck."

He fingered a lone orchid—incongruously placed in a plain glass vase—just like the one Cassandra had picked on her first morning in Parata Bay.

She came through with two cups and placed them on the small table between them. She folded her hands in her lap and sat tall, again to hide her stomach, he supposed.

"I'm surprised you'd say that. I imagined the only thing you think I deserve is to be charged with fraud." She took a sip of her herbal tea. For all her composure, Dallas noticed her hands were shaking slightly.

"You didn't carry out any fraud. Only prepared to do so."

"And you're not furious?"

"I was. But not now. Not now I know why."

She jumped in her seat and hot tea spilled onto her hand. Dallas shot forward and took the cup from her trembling hands. "You okay?"

"Fine. I'm fine." Absently, she rubbed her hands together. "What is it that you know?"

"Everything. About who you really are, your family's company, your father. And about Danny."

She pursed her lips, as if for control. "I see." She hesitated, looking down at her hands that wrung lightly in her lap. "I believed you to be responsible for the decision to take over the company, for my father's death and for Danny's..."

"No. My father made a bad decision. I tried to make the best of a bad job. I'm sorry for what happened."

"And I'm sorry, Dallas." She looked up at him, with tears in her eyes. "I'm so sorry. I was just so mad. So grieving. I wanted to hit out and you were the target."

He reached over for the first time and took her hands in his. "Grief twists reality. How do you feel now?"

Her eyes were fixed on their joint hands: hers encased in both of his. "I'm not angry any more." She half-laughed and glanced at him briefly. "I just feel guilty."

"No. How do you feel now about your loss? About losing Danny?"

He could have wept at the strange combination of sheer sadness and solid strength in her eyes. Only Cassandra had the character to come through such heartache without rejecting it completely. It was easy *not* to feel anything if you cut yourself off from it. But Cassandra hadn't done that. He could see it in her eyes. Her eyes and heart still held her son and her sadness, but he could see a strength and determination to move forward.

"I feel closer to Danny than I've felt since he went missing." She glanced at her stomach and then away. "It's hard to describe."

"Perhaps it's something to do with your pregnancy."

She looked up suddenly, her large eyes full of shock.

"You know?"

"Only since I watched you from outside. When's the baby due?"

"Wondering who the father is?"

The sudden bitterness of her tone cut him. "No. It's me, of course. Even if it wasn't, I don't care. I want to be a father to the child."

"Yes, right." Again the bitter, sarcastic tone.

"I do. Will you let me be the child's father?"

"Why would you want to do that Dallas? I've acted unforgivably to you."

"There's nothing to forgive." He pulled her hands to his lips and kissed her tight fists. "It's me and my family who need your forgiveness for setting in train the events that led to your father's suicide and the death of your child." She looked up at his face then, as a tear tracked its hot course down her cheek. "I'm so sorry, Cassandra. For everything." He reached down and kissed away the tear from her cheek, before kissing each eyelid. He tilted her chin and brought his lips close to hers, his eyes searching hers for an answer. "Forgive me?"

She paused only a moment before jerkily, imperceptibly nodding her head once. "It wasn't your fault, Dallas. If anyone's, it was my father's, it was mine. He'd been depressed for some time. I just hadn't realized how much. I shouldn't have let Danny go with him."

"No 'should haves' or 'shouldn't haves'. It's too late for that. There's only now and we have the future before us. Marry me, Cassandra."

His eyes flickered over her lips that tried to form a word, but hesitated. Then he looked back into her eyes where he saw her answer. She shook her head to confirm it. "No."

He pulled away. "Why not?"

"Not like this. Not out of a feeling of responsibility. I know you want to do the right thing. And I know that you've never wanted marriage or children. Why do you want me now?"

Dallas's heart pumped deeply, pounding, trying to push the words that refused to budge into his mouth.

"I want you. I want our child."

"We're not another business acquisition. You need to do more than 'want'."

"I want to marry you, be a father to your child. Isn't that enough?"

She slumped her forehead against his and he felt it roll from side to side as she shook her head. "No, it's not." Slowly she pulled away. "Not enough to build a life on. Guilt, responsibility, they're not enough to build a life on. I tried once, with my first husband, to build a marriage without love. It didn't work."

A shot of jealousy filled Dallas. "Don't compare me to anyone else."

"I'm not. You are"—she raised an eyebrow—"*incompa-rable*, Mr. Mackenzie."

"Glad to hear it."

"But it's still not enough."

It was like a hot knot working up from his gut, through his chest. He hadn't known anything like this pain, this feeling he would explode with emotion. "It *is* enough." He tried to keep his voice from shaking. "Come back with me to Wellington."

"No, Dallas. I have a life here. I don't want to be wanted out of a sense of duty."

"You're not."

"Then why do you want me?"

"Because... I can't easily explain."

"It's not hard if you know the words." Her voice was gentle. She stood up, pulling her hands away. "I understand, probably more than you know. I told you once that I thought you were scared. I think you still are. Until you know the words, I think you'd better go. Leave me here, where I've found a place I can be happy..." She bit her lip as if to try to retract the last word.

He stepped back as if dealt a blow. "You're happy here then..."

His fingers moved from hers. He held his hand in mid air for a split second as he watched her hand fall back to her side. He thrust his hands back in his pockets and turned away. It hurt too much. But it was hard. *Too hard.* For the first time in his life he felt lost, unable to frame the words that could lead the way for him.

She was right. He couldn't come to her like this, disrupting a life with which she was so obviously content. Not when his heart and mind raged with a fury which scared him.

He'd done his best to control the temper he'd inherited from his father. And, in so doing, he'd contained everything else too—all feeling. He couldn't open up to her now. Because God only knew what he'd be unleashing. She was right. He *was* still scared. And until he wasn't, he had no right to ask her to be with him.

"Go, Dallas. Thank you for coming, for your forgiveness. But you need to go now. There's nothing more to be said."

He shook his head, his eyes focused on the lone orchid.

Her eyes followed his. "It was Danny's favorite." He nodded, suddenly understanding. "He'd always loved them. He couldn't believe they grew wild, they looked so exotic. He used to dream of going to Bali to see the orchids we'd read about that grew wild there."

"I'm so sorry, Cassandra."

She shook her head jerkily and turned away from him. He could see the tension in her shoulders, her back, in the delicate line of her jaw that was tilted up defiantly as she waited for him to go.

He turned away and opened the door, the jingle of the bells ringing only once because he couldn't step through the threshold. As he gazed out at the trees opposite, their branches bare and stark under the winter sun, all he could see, all he could feel was emptiness. Life without Cassandra was untenable. It was no life. Six months ago, before Cassandra had entered his life, he'd looked out at the world and felt emptiness. Now there was no longer emptiness, so long as Cassandra was with him.

The door jangled once more as the door closed.

·  ·  ·

Cassandra felt the energy drain out of her body as the door rattled shut. He'd gone. She'd never see him again. She was filled with utter devastation as she slumped against the counter. She loved him but she refused to settle for anything less than love in return. Even if she didn't deserve it, her baby did. Their child didn't deserve a distant father, only doing his duty. She, or he, needed love—first and foremost. Her hands slid protectively around her stomach.

Suddenly she stopped moving. Her skin prickled with awareness and she closed her eyes, gathering her strength before turning around. "You didn't leave." Her eyes swept his body, taking in the uncompromising lines of his face, the curls of his hair, now longer than she'd ever seen it.

"No, I can't."

He looked so distressed, she wanted to go to him. The anguish in his eyes revealed the fight that was raging inside him. He held up his hand as she started forward.

"Don't come any closer, Cassandra. If you do, I won't be able to think at all."

She gripped the counter, willing herself to stay where she was, when all she wanted to do was to go to him. But she couldn't go to him. He had to do this alone. She knew he had to dig deep to find the words that would open up a part of himself that he'd been denying for so long.

He paced across the room and back to the door once more. "You know me." His tone was almost angry. "You know I've fought all my life against my father, against the frustration and anger that I've held close for so long." He thrust his hands into his pockets and looked at her under a lowering brow as if desperate to control the passions that she could see raged inside.

"I know—"

He held up his hand. "Let me say what I need to say,

Cassandra. You're right. Of course I'm scared to let it go and let myself love you. But it seems I have no choice. Because I can't leave here without you. I can't *live* without you." He looked up into her eyes with an expression so intense, so full of vulnerability, that her heart ached. "I do love you, Cassandra. So much that it scares me."

She was with him an instant, her hands moving around his body, pulling him to her for comfort. Except it wasn't Dallas that needed the comfort. It was her body that was shaking, it was her tears that soaked into his shirt. But it was his arms that curved around her body and supported her.

She felt the touch of his lips on the top of her head, felt the power of his arms and body supporting her and felt his love for her, like never before.

"Marry me, Cassandra?"

He pulled away and kissed her forehead and brushed away her tears with his thumbs, his hands cradling her face as if it were the dearest thing in the world to him.

The palm of his hands slid against her soft cheeks as she nodded, her heart too full to form the words, her lips to intent on finding his own lips to utter the words that would seal their future together. Instead, she let her body answer for her.

# EPILOGUE

"You've got to let Lily do it by herself!"

Cassandra laughed as Dallas only just managed to stop himself from taking the plump little toddler's hand into his own as she stumbled unsteadily towards the swings at the centre of Mackenzie Square. He folded his arms and watched as Lily picked up speed, sensing freedom was close, until she finally fell onto the soft surface. He was beside her in a moment and swept her up in his arms until she was giggling uncontrollably.

As Dallas brought Lily back to the bench where Cassandra sat, she considered, not for the first time, the similarity between them. Not in looks—she was the image of Cassandra—but in the direct gaze, the stubborn spirit and in her zest for life.

"I hope the next one isn't so feisty," he said cupping Cassandra's barely-showing stomach with one hand as he struggled to hold onto his young daughter with the other.

"Probably will be, with parents like us."

It was his turn to laugh. He drew Lily to him and landed a kiss on her curly head. She twisted her head up and grabbed his hair and gave him a very juicy sounding kiss. "Dada."

Cassandra hadn't known that someone could visibly melt before her eyes. But Dallas did. He allowed Lily to wriggle free of his grip and toddle off to the swings.

"I will love them all, whatever they're like, just as I love their mother." He kissed Cassandra lightly with lips that now curved into an easy smile before he jumped up and followed Lily to help her into a swing.

The sight of this powerful man, putty in the hands of his little girl, filled Cassandra with love.

Her hands instinctively found the small orchid that she'd pinned to her top and caressed its luscious petals. Dallas bought her an orchid every day.

Danny's flower.

He'd always be with her. Never forgotten. A part of their family, always.

# AFTERWORD

Thank you for reading *Secrets at Parata Bay*. I hope you enjoyed it. *Secrets at Parata Bay* is the second book in The Mackenzies series. An excerpt follows of the next book in the series—*Escape to Shelter Springs*—which features Callum and Gemma. The Mackenzies series consists of:

A Place Called Home (Guy and Lucia)
Secrets at Parata Bay (Dallas and Cassandra)
Escape to Shelter Springs (Callum and Gemma)
What you See in the Stars (Morgan and Rebecca)
Second Chance at Whisper Creek (James and Susie)
Summer at the Lakehouse Café (Pete and Lizzi)

Happy reading!

Sophie

# ESCAPE TO SHELTER SPRINGS
## BOOK 3 OF THE MACKENZIES—CALLUM

**A woman wanting freedom. A man determined to keep his family safe and secure. A marriage doomed before it's begun...**

*"A shepherd's hut, twenty-four hours, a stranger..." It's not the*

*perfect start to Gemma Winters' new life--another man is the last thing she needs after the suffocating control of her ex. But this man proves hard to resist!*

*Callum Mackenzie blames himself for his wife's death—he should have taken better care of her. So, when a one-night stand with a beautiful red-head has consequences, he's determined to make sure both she, and their baby, are looked after and safe.*

*That means marriage and two people forced to face their deepest fears...*

### Excerpt

They drove on towards the hills, overshadowed by the Southern Alps and entered a valley high above the surrounding plains, Gemma noticed the land wasn't so wild. Fences and small houses dotted the landscape. She sat forward and blinked her eyes in surprise as she peered into the distance.

Framed by tall trees behind, and a smooth lake that acted like a mirror in front, was a sprawling two-story nineteenth-century mansion, complete with not one but two ivy-covered towers that flanked the porticoed entrance.

"Wow! What's that?"

"Glencoe."

"It's huge." They drove around the lake, up an avenue of lime trees, their vivid green leaves flashing bright in the late sun. Around the house were dotted buildings, houses, farm offices. It was like a small village. "You work here?"

He glanced at her. "Yes."

"Pretty amazing house. Are its owners as snobby as the house looks?"

"Some of them."

"Oh well. I guess it's worth putting up with people like that to live in this place. It's beautiful."

"Yes, my thoughts exactly."

She looked around. The houses where, no doubt, the workers lived appeared well kept and comfortable, if a little small. "Which house do you live in?"

Callum swung the car around the top of the drive and pulled up beside the front door which was as imposing as the rest of the house with its pillars and wide steps down to the drive.

"This one." He pulled on the handbrake, cut the engine and grinned. "Glencoe."

"But..." She frowned. "Don't they mind? Having the workers stay in the house?"

His gaze drifted to her hair, which he pushed back while stroking his thumb down the side of her cheek. "They've made an exception in my case."

"Really?" She grinned back, teasing. "Because you're so tall and strong and handsome?"

"That, and because I own the place."

Find out more!

# ABOUT THE AUTHOR

Hello!

My name is Sophie Haydon and I write romances with stories which make you turn the pages, and characters who feel real.

I'm an avid people watcher, hopeless romantic and dreamer who spends far too much time gazing out the window, imagining scenes where people struggle with life and emotions but always end up happily. Because, yes, I'm also an eternal optimist!

I currently have two connected series — Mackenzies and Lantern Bay — which feature the Mackenzie and Connelly families. At the moment, I'm writing the fifth Lantern Bay book, but am already planning future series.

All the books I've written so far are set in New Zealand, where I live. But I was born on the north Norfolk coast of England and am planning a series set in the small seaside town in which I grew up. And then there's my Nantucket trilogy which I began planning years ago, but have yet to find time to write.

So, wherever you are in the world, welcome to my little corner, where I sit with my two cocker spaniels snoring gently beside me, creating worlds where people struggle with life and emotions but are always rewarded with love and happiness in the end. Because that's non negotiable!

I hope you enjoy my books.

Sophie

x

## ALSO BY SOPHIE HAYDON

### *The Mackenzies*

A Place Called Home

Secrets at Parata Bay

Escape to Shelter Springs

What you See in the Stars

Second Chance at Whisper Creek

Summer at the Lakehouse Café

### *Lantern Bay*

Yours to Give

Yours to Treasure

Yours to Cherish

Yours to Keep

Yours Forever

Yours to Love

www.ingramcontent.com/pod-product-compliance
Lightning Source LLC
Chambersburg PA
CBHW022153240626
47153CB00007B/2646